Photo credit: Danielle Binks

Award-winning writer Merlinda Bobis writes in three languages across multiple genres. Her works have received literary recognition in Australia, Philippines, USA, and Italy. She has performed her dramatic works at various international venues. About her creative process, she writes: 'Writing visits like grace. In an inspired moment we almost believe that anguish can be made bearable and injustice can be overturned, because they can be named. And if we're lucky, joy can even be multiplied, so we may have reserves in the cupboard for the lean times.'

www.merlindabobis.com.au

Other books by Merlinda Bobis

Fish-Hair Woman
(2012)

The Solemn Lantern Maker
(2008, 2009)

Banana Heart Summer
(2005, 2008)

Pag-uli, Pag-uwi, Homecoming
(2004)

White Turtle
(1999, 2013)

Summer was a Fast Train without Terminals
(1998)

Cantata of the Warrior Woman Daragang Magayon/
Kantada ng Babaing Mandirigma Daragang Magayon
(1993, 1997)

Ang Lipad ay Awit sa Apat na Hangin/
Flight is Song on Four Winds
(1990)

Rituals
(1990)

LOCUST GIRL

a lovesong

MERLINDA BOBIS

First published by Spinifex Press, 2015
Reprinted 2016 (twice), 2018

Spinifex Press Pty Ltd
PO Box 5270, North Geelong, Victoria 3215
PO Box 105, Mission Beach, Queensland 4852
Australia
women@spinifexpress.com.au
www.spinifexpress.com.au

Cover design: Deb Snibson
Typesetting: Helen Christie
Typeset in Albertina Std
Printed by McPherson's Printing Group

National Library of Australia Cataloguing-in-Publication data:

Bobis, Merlinda C. (Merlinda Carullo), author.
Locust girl : a lovesong / Merlinda Bobis

9781742199627 (paperback)
9781742199597 (ebook : epub)
9781742199573 (ebook : pdf)
9781742199580 (ebook : Kindle)

Climatic changes—Fiction.
Environmental refugees—Fiction.
Food security—Fiction.
Human ecology—Fiction.
Social ecology—Fiction.
Fantasy fiction.

A823.3

ACKNOWLEDGMENTS

I wish to thank Spinifex Press for all their years of conviction, passion, and kindness. Thanks to Susan Hawthorne, Renate Klein, and Pauline Hopkins for their keen eyes and heart in the editing of this book, and for hearing the songs of Locust Girl; to Deb Snibson for visualising them in the cover design; to Helen Christie for setting them on the page; to all the places and people in Wollongong, Canberra, and Legazpi that nurtured the dreaming up of this book in all its strangeness; to my family for always believing; and to Reinis Kalnins for the enduring love that makes me sing.

For those walking to the border for dear life
And those guarding the border for dear life

Even if your worst enemy is thirsty and he asks for water,
you have to give him a cup of water,
because they believed, and we still believe
that water is life and water gives peace.

Rudolf Dâusab of The Namib Desert

(*Extremes: Survival in the Great Deserts of the Southern Hemisphere*
National Museum of Australia, 2005–2006)

LOCUST GIRL

Once upon a time

*

I was nine when the stars went out. When the sky was taught a lesson: no one should shine or outshine anyone. All must know darkness and light must be rationed equally. We were warned on the box, a tiny blue square that kept us hoping, kept us on the line. Our tents were also blue like water and rationed. We lived in the desert of many tents. Our halfway homes between heaven and earth, the blue box said, so we should be grateful. The sun and wind rippled the blue cloth and we thought, water! And drank up the thought.

I'd just had dinner when the stars went out. Sand porridge and locust. Good for protein, the blue box said. The locust crackled between my teeth. I was in my blue dress, also rationed like the number and letter inscribed just beneath my right ear: 425a in blue ink. I was the daughter of number 425 living in tent 425, where there was no 425b or c or d. I was his only daughter and I did not have a mother. She would have been (425), a creature forever hidden like all the other mothers whom I hardly saw. But I knew they were around, their arms a warm pillow for their sons and daughters on cold nights. Or a shade for their eyes when the desert sun soared too high as if to abandon the horizon forever.

No pillow or shade for me but I did not complain. I promised myself one day I'll soar with the sun or I'll walk to the horizon and sink to the other side. Such was my thought before the stars went out. Before my father Abarama went to walk under their distant lights. He said walking under the stars was good for digestion. He took two mouthfuls of his sand porridge but did not touch the locust, then he walked off so the meal could settle nicely in his belly. He limped out of the tent, saying, 'Finish my dinner, Amedea. I've had too much and I must have my digestive promenade.' My father had a way with words.

I grabbed his bowl and ate his meal, having licked my own bowl clean. I crunched his share of locust, trying to convince myself I'd be full. My father believed little bellies must be treated well, so they can grow into big, strong, and good bellies. 'Mine has no more room to grow, so I'm all right.' Nightly he gave up his dinner for me.

I knew it was a beautiful night from the wedge of deep blue outside where I last saw my father. It was a clear sky. I knew he would have plenty of stars to ease his belly. From where I sat finishing his meal, I caught a glimpse of his bad leg dragging behind. It was flattened and pushed inwards from the knee to the ankle. 'Because of too much dancing with beautiful ladies. You see, my dear Amedea, this leg remembers, like trees bent this way or that forever because of the wind. Even if there's no more wind.' He winked at me and I winked back. My father and I understood each other.

'Beautiful ladies with the scent of wind behind their ears and that of sand on the hollows of their throat. And trees, a multitude of trees.'

'But what's trees, Father?'

'Tall things with leaves.'

'What's leaves?'

'Green things.'

'What's green?'

My father frowned deeply to squeeze from his brow the apparition of trees for me. 'Green was tall and proud. Ah, dear daughter, once upon a time there were trees standing proudly like beautiful ladies.'

Was my mother as proud as a tree? And how beautiful? Tell me about trees, father. Tell me about mother.

'Alkesta … as beautiful as a tree,' he muttered under his breath.

'Tell me more,' I begged but he had already stood up, ready to walk under the stars as he'd always done each night. So I never knew my mother beyond a whispered name. Alkesta. My queries for stories about her, about trees, about his dance with them, about when the dancing stopped, and about his mangled leg had grown fat only at the tip of my tongue. Even before I learned how to walk, he and I had understood each other. There were 'no-go-no-story zones' between us. There were silences.

But that night when the stars went out, when I last saw my father, it was not silent. Through five hundred blue tents turned black in the dark, there was the rustle of hundreds of scraping spoons and tongues licking bowls. It was a simmering down sound, settling down like bellies for the night. For the dream of bigger and better rations the next day or maybe the next. No, for the rations to arrive. They had stopped coming for a month. Our hungry mouths were gnawing at top sand, worrying the earth, and the grey, underground locusts were burrowing too deep beyond our reach.

Soon the tapping of spoons on bowls began, calling for the fathers to walk together under the stars after dinner. I licked my father's bowl and licked mine again, and heard a song that played like a rumour in my head.

Abarama, tell me the story
Again please but with no silences
Amedea, tell Abarama's story
Again please but sing the silences

*

The grey locusts had bulging blue eyes and blue whiskers. Like strange prawns, my father said. He knew prawns from long ago, but not me. I had never seen prawns or the water where they were found. Water which he called riverrrr, with a delicate roar in his mouth, or ocean, with a ssshh that hushed me to sleep. My father had seen all those 'big, big waters, sometimes as big as this desert and coloured blue.' I could not imagine them, especially when he said you couldn't drink them, well the salty ones. I only knew water from the blue barrels rationed from far away, way past the horizon.

Long ago he had eaten pink prawns that looked like locusts. 'Well sort of, only normal,' he said, while sucking his tongue. He ate prawns as a young man dancing with beautiful ladies.

Finally I cracked the locust head, saved under my tongue as my last mouthful, and imagined the blue eyes bursting and turning pink. A shade lighter than what comes out of you if you prick yourself, my father said. Then I wiped the two bowls with the hem of my dress, lay them upside down beside the two spoons at the foot of my mat and turned off the blue flame. It was also rationed in tiny glass vials that looked pretty and useless. The light was too small, too dim. We were on our last light. Tomorrow night we would have to eat in the dark. If we could find enough top sand, the finer kind, and if we could trick the locusts out of hiding.

The tapping of spoons on bowls continued. In the dark I imagined my father walking. He won't be back till early morning, till the last star closed its eye. I was not to wait for him. 'Just sleep tight so you can grow up big and strong and good.' Thus my father sighed whenever he looked at me.

I sighed too before I lay on the mat that night. Under my lids

I walked with my father. I imagined we walked far, close to the horizon, but never touching it. Then we came back as he always did, for where else could he go?

I could not sleep. I turned towards the wedge of sky outside, now black, not daring to open the tent a little bit more. I did not wish to see the dragging leg and doubt his dance with beautiful ladies. They must remain tall and proud in the arms of a young man turning on two good legs.

Up in the sky I saw three stars forming an upside down V. Like the peak of a tower, he used to say. Father had seen towers. 'These you will see for yourself when you grow up, when the right time comes. But it's not yet the right time, so promise me to sleep tight and to grow up big and strong and good.' I forced myself to keep my promise, though I cheated for a while. I etched the three shining points under my lids and saw towers lulled by the rustle of the night. In the other tents meals were just drawing to a close.

Finally the scraping of spoons faded.

Then the licking of tongues on bowls.

And the wind rose, flapping the five hundred tents.

And the blue box sang. About stars, about stars resting. About rest for one night. *For our last night.*

Who could have heard that warning? Rest with a long, soft sssss. We thought it was our breathing, the hum of our dreams.

'Amedeaaaaaaaaa — Amedeaaaaaaaaa!'

Did I dream that too, his cry, before the stars burned brighter? Lights, lights! A shower of them dropped on our tents, our mats, our bowls, our spoons. They afflicted our eyes, our ears, our tongues, our noses, our skin with their song. Lights, roaring lights. Blinding lights. Not rationed for once. We had our fill.

Did I dream such abundance? Such searing heat?

They shot down the stars
They shot down the stars
They shot down the stars
They shot down the stars

☆

Black. The sky. The desert. And tents 1 to 500. All the colour of cinder. But I was not to know until ten years later. A hundred feet beneath the ground, my eyes were shut. I was keeping my promise to my father. I was sleeping.

☆

They were small, snug and hidden. They ate grains as we did. Then the grains dried up so they ate sand. Then we ate them and sand. Then they ate their eaters. They gorged. We were five hundred families after all. So they burst like pods that could not hold their seams together.

Did I dream this?

The charred bodies above the ground saved me. I was buried too deep, too hidden. Like the locusts before they clambered out after the silence and nibbled at the dead, inquiringly at first. Did I dream this too? And the fire that plunged through the roof of tent 425? Then through the two bowls and a hundred feet below where it exploded and cleared a bed for me. Small and snug and hidden.

In my bed or burial ground I dreamt again and again about my father walking but never reaching the horizon. Always I walked behind him, except when we reached the edge where

I walked past him and fell to the other side, still wondering if he had digested his dinner. Dinner was glittering bowls of pink prawns. I was sure we had finished them with much relish. We were so full, we did not have to lick our bowls. It was our best meal ever, but I'm sure we had to eat in the dark. The rationed blue vials of light had exploded and the stars were all gone. The sky had been levelled black. Up there, no one outshining the other. Down here, all equally sheltered by the dark.

In the dark, in my dream, something nibbled at my skin crusted black. A falling star had burnt me. I dreamt this too? The nibbling thing was the last of the grey underground creatures with once blue eyes and whiskers. It had turned black like me and could not clamber out. It could not feast above the ground and so was saved. It was dislodged from its nest by the explosion and had fallen into a deeper hole with me. Trapped, it had grown confused, forgetting how to feed. It nibbled at me, thinking I was a stone blocking its way. It nibbled parts of my burnt crust in patches. Then it grew tired. It nibbled its way under my forehead and there slept my ten-year sleep.

We listen to the other's dreams
In the other's skin — once a locust
And a girl, then a locust girl
Dreaming a single dream

☆

Beenabe told me she had never seen black and white earth before. She only knew brown. She only knew desert. It was her home and now she had strayed from it. She had been walking for five days. She was tired and thirsty, but hunger she managed well at first. She nibbled the grains of barley in her pocket.

In her own home desert, from the highest peak that no one was allowed to climb lest they looked beyond the horizon, she had made out something dark and light from afar. Something not quite the colours she knew. She had looked once, only once, but she had looked hard and long. At least long enough before anyone noticed that she was up there, spying for something beyond the edge.

No one should look

No one should walk beyond the horizon

From far away, in a place unknown even to our dreams, the Five Kingdoms issued these laws. The Minister of Mouths sang them every morning in the orange box, the brightest thing in Beenabe's hut of clay. Then he ended his song with an attribution. The song was composed by the Minister of Legs who wrote all the songs of transport and passage: of walking and even running, of how and where you can walk or run, of all the to-ings and fro-ings in the world.

The orange box was so orange, like the late sun or the deepest shade of the desert before the Five Kingdoms neutralised all colours with ochre rain: simplify, no bright tones. Bright tones make the eyes wish for more brightness and this is not healthy, so the Minister of Mouths sang.

The ochre rain turned the sun and sky to ochre. It made hair fall out and stomachs shrink. It was rumoured to be cost-saving rain. The Kingdoms did not have to supply lice poison any more or the usual amount of barley and water.

Beenabe was convinced she lived in dull monochrome: all hues of brown. Fancy ochre, hah! Thankfully there was the orange box, which everyone treasured because it was a big leap from drab brown. Orange was a concession, so Beenabe's people would listen to The Songs. The Honourable Head thought with cleverness:

What the eyes treasure, the ears treasure

More clever was the gift of the word *ochre*. Shade of the desert. After brainstorming with his ministers, the Honourable Head wisely decided that all must blend with their habitat as animals would.

For symmetry. For equality. For justice.

He thought in grand leaps. Thus everything was rationed in ochre that's just like the sand, the sky. The Minister of Mouths said it was a more colourful word than *brown*. So ochre it was, even the water barrels. And of course barley was ochre, he decided.

The orange box was light on Beenabe's palm but singing weighty words: '*No one should look. No one should walk beyond the horizon.*' She knew that the note was heaviest in the word *No*. What ear could mistake such a warning, but she had grown too curious for her own sake. Her eyes ached at night, then her chest. Because after that furtive climb to the forbidden peak, under her lids she kept seeing those new colours from afar: black and white. They seeped into her heart and she dreamt of walking to the edge of her village. But she always came back in the morning, for where else could she go?

She was hot now, the sun baking what was not covered by her wrap the colour of dung. All the women wore the same colour and secretly hated it. Beenabe was sixteen, the eldest of three girls, and she hated it most. Dung! The other women whispered about how long ago before she was born, there were other shades so bright, they hurt the eyes in a wonderful way. Blue birds against the yellow sun. Red buds on green cactus. Before the ochre rain.

Amid the miles of burning brown Beenabe adjusted her wrap so it covered her head, which felt like it would burst under the heat. How would it be to have blue hair and red cheeks and green lips? She only knew red when she pricked herself and the sky could never be blue again after the ochre rain. And she did not know green of course, nor had she known hair.

Her sisters said she was vain. Often they caught her admiring her reflection in the monthly barrel of water. The truth was she was scolding herself for being so drab. So she took to the habit of holding the orange box close to her face to brighten it and her family forgave her vanity. Of course she's listening to The Songs all the time.

She had slipped the box into her pocket with two fistfuls of barley before she left. To go walking, she told her sisters who both frowned and said, 'But you have to get back before the sun sets, to cook dinner.'

'It's your turn to cook dinner, I cook it every day,' Beenabe protested.

'But the orange box sings that the eldest girl should cook dinner.'

Beenabe stroked the box in her pocket and smirked. 'You heard it wrong. What do you know about The Songs? I listen to them every day.'

'We'll tell on you to father and mother,' the younger girls chorused.

'And where are they?'

'Queuing for rations, where else.'

Beenabe refused to queue and her parents always wrung their hands, exasperated with her arrogance. But Beenabe simply walked away from all censure. Surely there's something more to life than queuing for the benevolence of the Five Kingdoms. She hated waiting. She wanted to take charge of her own hunger. So she walked when her parents were away. They tolerated her truancy but only because of her nose for food. She had a way of scavenging for odd bits and pieces for the stomach, something to make the barley taste more than barley, something strange and sometimes quite special. Beenabe was bravely enterprising. She walked, she gathered, and returned with gifts. Maybe today she could walk further. Stray a bit. Find new colours, new tastes, who knows.

If the feet itch for distance
Does the head know?
If the eyes spy colour
Do the legs go — weak?

*

The black grew blacker, the white whiter. Beenabe told me that before she knew their names, these colours had already seeped into her eyes, her heart, her head. All hurt but her heart hurt more, as if a hand were squeezing it at each step. What desert is this? Is this desert? She stopped chewing the barley grain then she stopped her feet. Or her feet stopped her, her feet were afraid. But Beenabe had always been too curious for her own sake. Four hundred paces more and she would know. She had learned how to measure distance with her paces.

It was a colour darker than the night, even the darkest night. Then a splash here and there of something light. It was actually white. A whiteness not flat like the black but shaping themselves in her eyes as she drew closer. The hand tightened around her heart and her head throbbed. The sun leapt around what looked like white sticks and balls, hundreds of them, some piled together like kindling, but mostly laid out in smaller numbers as if someone had sorted them into sets. And in the foreground, matching the length of the horizon, was a line of them, the balls with holes and the sticks linked in rhythmic patterns.

Fifty paces, twenty paces, and still Beenabe refused to believe what she saw. Pictures from her wanderings came and went in her head: the remains of a jaw of some creature, the burnished bones of a rodent, once perhaps a boy who had wandered too far from home, and it made her weep. Now she felt faint, her knees giving way, her mouth opening and closing, but she had lost her voice. This can't be, this can't be.

Black earth and white bones! As far as the eyes can see, as far as a lifetime of paces. Paces beyond her counting.

How the sun leapt on the skulls staring at the girl who had forgotten how to shut her mouth.

☆

She had fallen on something sharp, but she did not even notice that her hands and knees were bleeding. She was held by the gaze of a skull leaning against half a rib, mouth opened just so. Beenabe thought it was asking her a question. She stared back for a long time.

'No one should look

No one should walk beyond the horizon'

Beenabe jumped up at hearing the song from her pocket. She remembered the orange box and suddenly felt the urge to run. The notes were scolding her. She tried to muffle the box with her fist, but of course it must run its ten-minute course. She held it in a panic, wondering if anyone else was hearing this, then remembered she was the only one here, alive that is. The box kept up its song. She held it out to the skull as if to explain and say 'sorry.' Only then did she notice her bleeding hands.

My blood is brighter than the orange box, she thought as

the skull looked on. She noticed too her bleeding knees and the drops of red on the black earth where she finally discovered the culprit. A half-buried barbed wire running for miles, alongside the line of skulls and bones. She understood. They were about to cross, to walk to the horizon and beyond.

By the time Beenabe had accepted the reality of her discovery, she was calmer. She squatted a few paces from where she bled, face turned away from the plains of black and white. The sight squeezed her heart too much, she couldn't breathe. She turned towards where she had walked from. Home.

Since she left two days ago, the horizon had bothered her immensely, far more than her thirst. That edge, that long line, which she wanted to cross, was always beyond home, wasn't it? The sun always sank into that line, but now it seemed to be sinking into where she came from. Could home be the horizon then? How come? Or did she really understand where the horizon was? Was it beyond her or behind her?

Maybe the Minister of Mouths was lying. Maybe he himself had never walked away from home. How could he? He was trapped in the orange box.

Maybe the Honourable Head had thought out this trick, knowing there could be strays like her.

Maybe she was too thirsty, her eyes had begun to lie to her. Beyond the horizon, there were only skulls and bones?

Or maybe she was lost. She had stopped counting her paces yesterday. Her paces were too many and beyond the numbers that she could count in her head and no one could help her. She had never felt so alone in all of her sixteen years. So alone among the skulls and bones of five hundred families, but she did not know this yet. Not until I told her of my dream.

Dream me hundreds of skulls and bones
Beyond your horizon

Eyes staring just so, mouths opened just so
Beyond your ken

*

It was the whirring that woke her. It was midnight, but how could she know this? This was a place with no stars or moon. She had never seen night this desolate and inhospitable.

She groped for the orange box in her pocket. It was not throbbing. The whirring was from somewhere else. Or someone else? She grew both hopeful and afraid and did not like the feeling, so she clamped her ears with her hands and curled into an even tighter ball. It was not only too dark but also too cold. It was the darkest night that she'd ever seen. As if one could even see in this dark. She wondered about the empty sky. What place is this? What place has no stars or moon? Will she ever get home again to a lit sky, to a hut of clay or hot barley soup, to her sisters' warmth on their shared bed, even to her parents' scolding? Better than this, better than this.

The whirring grew louder, boring into her ear, urging her to her feet. It spurred her to action and forced the course of her limbs. She stood up, urged to face again the plains of black and white where the whirring was coming from, urged to cross beyond the spot where she bled, to wade through the skulls and bones. Only balls and sticks, she told herself so she could push on with the next step, her bare feet feeling hardness, sharpness, brittleness, the rolling or crunching, the crashing or crackle of kindling. Yes, think kindling, only kindling, like what she had scavenged from ruins whenever she strayed from home.

The whirring was like a singing now. It had highs and lows, and meandered through a scale. After a while it grew melodic, small notes in a wordless ditty. It afflicted not only her legs but also her arms as she tumbled and sank into piles of kindling and dug herself out again, so she could keep going. Her arms ached as the song pulled at them when she crashed into the deepest pile of all. Her arms urged her to dig up a clearing where the song was loudest. Her fingers were afflicted too, even her nails. They throbbed with a strange, delicious ache as the notes seeped into them while she dug on. In the morning maybe she would see song under her nails, like brown dirt when she scavenged for food underground.

Then she hit something softer, like sand but not dry like the desert she knew. The song stopped in her ears but its rhythm remained in her hands, making them tremble. She grabbed at a piece of kindling, yes, it's just kindling, she convinced herself, and began digging more furiously. She had to keep digging till the morning.

The sky was growing light when the whirring began again but faintly and in short bursts. Then she heard the short bursts echoed by another sound. Like someone digging from below but upwards. She stopped digging. The other digging stopped too. She laid her ear close to the earth and felt the strangest sensation. As if another ear had just been placed beneath hers. As if two ears were now listening to each other. She listened to the other's listening. Then the digging underneath began again. What is it? Beenabe felt a mixture of hope and fear. Something or someone else is here, alive like her. But soon the fear ate up the hope. She stopped digging altogether and stood up. She could see how deeply she had dug herself in. She felt the hole closing in on her. She could hear her heart pounding louder than the digging below.

Up there it was growing light and down here was all shadow. She stretched towards the circle of sky. Up there was safe. Maybe.

Underneath her feet Beenabe felt a frantic knocking and thrusting, as if *this something* down there knew she was about to abandon it. She tried to shut her ears. She began to clamber out of the hole, scolding herself for her foolish curiosity. Which was what got you into this hole, stupid girl, which was what led you astray. She fell back several times before she finally got out, her soles still tingling with the desperate rhythm underground.

Her eyes scanned the growing light. Where she came from was now almost visible or so she thought: home. She will go home. There are no gifts for scavengers beyond the edge. She knew that now. She leapt across the hole, eyes only on home, the *new* horizon.

That was how I first saw her. A flash of feet in midair.

Help. My first attempted word. I felt my lips crack apart, felt my breath on the H, and tried again. 'H-he— ' I heard the running footsteps stop, I sensed their uncertainty. I tried again. 'Hel— ' The footsteps rushed away, I heard crackling and crashing, as if someone had fallen over a pile of something. Then rolling and cries of alarm and more crashing, and something hurtling towards me and balls and sticks pouring down with the screaming and I wanted to scream with it but my throat was just finding itself and all I could say was a feeble, 'Help … plea—'

I could not finish. The rain of things, whatever they were, and this screaming had knocked the wind out of me.

Finally the raining stopped but the scream kept on. It was a girl, a screaming girl buried in balls and sticks with me. Screaming and eyes almost popping in terror at me. At me? She was pointing at my forehead which had begun to whirr, then she was crying, 'Don't hurt me, don't hurt me.'

I had to make sure I was not dreaming any more. Slowly I remembered how to peel my arms off me, I heard me crackle with the movement. An agonising recall of muscles and bones as I freed me from my own tight embrace to reach out and touch her cheek.

*

My inquiring touch. That set her off again. She set me off again. She screamed, my forehead whirred. By the time we stopped, the sky was lighter.

We were buried waist-deep in a deeper hole and facing each other, and long after we were silent, we were still too afraid to blink.

To stare is bad manners. Where did I hear that before? I tried to remember, so I said it, though it took me a long time to form the words.

'T-to — ssss-stare — is b-bad — bad.'

The girl was relieved to hear something close to her own tongue. Later she would tell me that all she heard at first was mumbling or growling, that she thought I was a wild animal with a light-dark face.

And a locust on the forehead.

'What are you?' she asked, shuddering.

Silence.

'Who are you?'

Silence. Because I could not remember.

'What's your name?'

'N-n—namm— ' I faltered on the word.

'Yes, name.'

I did not know what she meant.

'Name. Beenabe. That's my name,' she said pounding her chest, then, 'And you?'

'B-bee—na—be.'

'No, no. I'm Beenabe.'

'B-bee—Beena—be.'

'Yes, me Beenabe.'

'M-me—Bee—na—Bee-na-be.' I kept repeating and she kept protesting. She had grown braver with this altercation, which went on for the whole day with bouts of silence when she closed her eyes to shut out my face.

Finally she said, 'You don't know, do you — you don't have a name,' and she thought some more. 'How can anyone not have a name?'

I shook my head, trying to dislodge the fog. It was hard to explain about the fog of waking up after ten years and I did not even know yet that it was ten years.

'I will call you Beena then. Beena after me. Because I found you.'

The sun was setting when we had our first proper conversation. I thought my saviour Beenabe was giving me lessons in speech.

'F-found you,' I aped the movement of her lips.

'No, I found you,' she protested, impatient now. 'I found Beena.'

'F-found,' I tried again and tapped her cheek. 'Found Beena.'

This time, she did not scream. 'Yes,' she said and almost smiled, 'I found Beena.'

I stretched my lips like her.

*

Much later I would tell her, that's how to scare fear away when faced with a stranger. With talk. When we find words to exchange, our hearts will not pound too much.

In the hole I was too engrossed with finding my voice, I barely realised I could not move from waist down. Or maybe because I had forgotten how to move and what I could recall were the muscles of my face. As for Beenabe, she was only too relieved to find me human and alive, so she forgot about our being buried but only for a while.

'No one should look

No one should walk beyond the horizon'

I heard it, didn't I? Beenabe was singing, but her lips weren't moving? No they were saying something else — 'The orange box, the orange box!' — then she was digging furiously. 'Dig, Beena, find it — it's a square box bright as fire and it sings, it fits in the palm of the hand, can you see it, go on, dig, we have to dig it out, we have to dig us out, we have to get out of here, we have to get out!' she kept on, her voice breaking into a sob. She had broken the law, she had looked beyond the horizon and found a graveyard and she might be buried in it forever as punishment.

I was perplexed at this burst of fear but soon I stopped listening to her. I was looking around, needing to touch, to know things. But again my arms had wrapped around myself and it was agony to unwrap them, to hold for the first time the sticks and balls while the song kept up its warning against the horizon. I could not heed Beenabe's urging. I could not understand why my eyes felt watery and burning, why I hurt from chest to throat. I was looking at each stick closely, examining each ball, peering through its two holes and the third gaping one, wondering if the song was coming from in there. Then for the first time, I *saw* it, I *knew* it.

'H-head —'

'Shut up, Beena!'

'Head, head, head,' I tested the word over and over again, and Beenabe screamed in protest. 'Head, head, head' rolled on my tongue that itched to ask questions. Questions I didn't even know and wouldn't know until later. All I knew was the head was not singing and pressed against me, its mouth was hard and cold, and Beenabe was struggling to prise it from my grasp but I couldn't give it up. It was listening to my heart, I was listening to its lack of song. How could she take this shared listening away from us? Thus we struggled and the locust on my brow began to sing.

'The edge is a line, oh how lovely
It will stretch your eye
The edge is a line, oh how sharp
It will cut your feet'

*

So it came to pass that she escaped from the hole but without the orange box. I couldn't understand why anyone would weep over a box. She did not even look at me still trapped down there. My saviour had forgotten me, and she'd probably leave me. I could see a hint of her toes above, I could hear her anguish. This did not bother me as much as the object of her despair.

An orange box? Something was terribly wrong and I was trying to remember why. I shut my eyes, imagining the box in my head but its colour was wrong, wrong.

'It was the most beautiful thing that I ever owned,' she explained between sobs. 'Each family owns one in my village, to sing the laws, but it's not the singing that I've lost, Beena, but the orange, the only bright thing in my life.'

At that first meeting I sensed this was a girl whose tears were too close to the surface. A brave soul but given to damp moments which made me want to look away. After a while, I called out, 'O-or-ange?'

'Yes, yes, the brightest thing — '

'B-blue,' I whispered. On hearing this, she peered down at me. I could see only half of her face silhouetted against the dusk.

'You know *blue?*' she asked, incredulous.

How could I answer, I didn't even know where the word came from.

Then I saw it before I heard it — the shadow that fell upon me and the hole and Beenabe up there, I'm sure — then there was Beenabe falling back into the hole, like we were going to play our first meeting all over again. Then the whirring, louder than mine. So loud it was, I thought all the locusts of the earth had conspired to sing together or that a giant locust had flown over us. For that was the shadow, wasn't it?

There were no words to this giant's song and the whirring rested on a single note. There was no attempt at melody.

'There's something up there,' Beenabe whispered. 'In the sky.'

I don't remember how long we kept still but suddenly it was dark. This is what happens when there are no stars or moon. Darkness falls quickly, like a blow, and seems final. There will never be any light again.

Soon the whirring grew faint then it stopped and curiosity got the better of us. We had to look beyond the hole even if we could hardly see each other's face. Quietly we helped each other clamber out. We knew that whatever it was, the shadow had landed.

The whole time Beenabe held my hand.

☆

Lights, lights! The stars have returned! They've come down to earth!

From behind a mountain of skulls, we saw beams of light floating in the darkness but close to the ground. I wanted to rush into the open and welcome the return of the stars — they were lost, weren't they? My brow began to itch and I heard my own locust gearing up for a song. I clamped my hand over it — hush!

What was it about to sing?

They shot down the stars they shot down the stars — but I couldn't make sense of the song that I heard in my head nor of my thought that the stars have returned. We lost them, didn't we? Then all thoughts were lost again as Beenabe's hand gripped mine even tighter and kept me from rushing to the lights. We waited, our breaths held, as the beams came together.

After a while, we saw more clearly. There were two white bodies walking around, holding what looked like a circle of lights — white bodies with no faces! The skulls and bones were alive, the dead were walking! They were speaking in a foreign tongue, though Beenabe made out an old, old word. *Blessed.* It was the word for 'good earth', for rich loam where things can grow. It was an almost forgotten word in a time when everything had turned into uninhabitable dryness.

'Blessed,' one of them said again, then a tumble of strange words as the other cleared a section of the black earth and shone a light onto it. Afterwards, from his side he took out a glass thing the size of his finger then scooped bits of the earth. A whoop of joy followed. So like my father's when he discovered a nest of locusts. Father? I had a father? Vaguely I remembered, but all went blank again as the more talkative one picked up a tiny skull and slid it into what looked like a box. It lit up and trembled. When it was opened, I saw that the skull had disappeared. In its place was white powder also scooped with a little glass finger and held aloft, along with the other glass of black earth.

They shone their lights on the black and the white glasses, then poured their contents into a bigger glass. In an instant, it became the brightest light of all.

Then the word again, uttered with much reverence. 'Blessed!'

Then the laughter, and how joyful. In my head I heard another laughter from a man holding out a palmful of locusts to his only child.

'Oh to find a gift — is it really one?
Oh to believe in the find —
Is it worth the belief?
Oh to hold worth in the hand!'

She stared at my brow long before its song had ended, then whispered, 'Be scared of the living, not the dead.'

She sounded old.

The dead had disappeared by now, swallowed by a giant

locust that flew away with winking lights. It took me an hour to tell her what I thought I saw and for her to understand.

'Not locust or the dead, Beena,' she sighed as she dug a little hole for the remnants of the white powder. It was too dark to see now but I had kept my hand close to hers the whole time. We had groped our way to the clearing left by the men in white suits and masks. Beenabe explained them to me as she searched for *that* powder. Between my fingers, it felt like the finest sand. Head, head, head, pounded within my own skull. I saw it, didn't I, that tiny skull turned into powder in the box.

'Once I saw this boy, you know, just bits of him left … perhaps wandered too far from home — is this your *home,* Beena?'

The word sounded familiar, like something that lives inside your chest wherever you go. For this was how it felt when she said the word like a tender hum. But how could I answer when I did not know what it meant?

'*Home.* You don't know it? And *planes* too? That was a plane, not a locust. Planes fly with winking lights and drop ochre rain on your home, so you lose your bright colours and your children lose their hair and their stomachs shrink.'

I thought she was going to cry again so I squeezed her hand that was now patting the earth over the buried powder. Then I heard her fumble with her wrap. 'Here,' she said, pressing what felt like the tiniest pebble onto my hand. 'Barley. Chew it, it will make you feel better.'

This was another strange thing about my saviour. She felt better by making me feel better, but only on those early days.

She patted the earth again, then pushed her last grain of barley into it, whispering, 'Blessed indeed.' She thought I didn't hear, but I did. My brow did.

'Blessed are they whose bones don't sleep
They are guarding the living
Blessed are they whose homes don't sleep
They are guarding the dead'

*

It had been a freezing night. I woke up under her wrap, snugly cuddled. She would hold me thus many times in her sleep to keep warm, but she would never touch my face. I shifted, my back rubbing against her. How soft, especially the two mounds that pressed against my neck. I felt my own chest. How hard, rough and flat. I rubbed my ankles against her and found her knees. How small I was compared to my new friend who, last night, had promised to take me home. Her own home.

Beenabe was sixteen. I was nineteen in a nine-year old body.

'You fidget,' she muttered and soon was scrambling to her feet. The cave of bones under which we had slept the night before tumbled down, trying to bury me again.

'Let's get started, Beena. Soon it will be too hot to walk.'

Slowly I got up, my body still creaking with all these new movements. I was learning how to crawl out of burial, to get used to this resurrection.

Then I heard her cry of astonishment.

'You're *not* dressed!'

Finally in the morning light, I was exposed. How was I to know that my clothes had been burnt into my skin? Or worse, that I was not like her?

'You're *not* one colour!'

For the first time, I looked at all of me too, and yes, she was right. My body was patches of black, white and grey, partly burnt and partly pale in the parts that were nibbled by the locust before it slept in me. But how could I explain what I did not remember?

'Not *one* colour.' She shook her head in disbelief and instinctively rubbed her brown arms, perhaps assuring herself that she was smooth and evenly hued. She could not let the matter rest.

'Who where you born from? What happened to your father and mother? Don't you know you can't be like this? Don't you know this — this unevenness is dangerous?' For a while, she would skirt around the word "impure." 'Don't you know you can't walk with me like — like this?'

My head reeled with her questions. I could not understand any of them so how could I answer? I pointed to my hole a few metres away. All answers were buried there, so I heard in some far corner of my skull.

'No, I won't leave you back in there.' Her voice had softened. So did her face, as she noticed my distress. I wanted to turn my back on the huge sun now coming full circle and seeing what Beenabe saw: I am impure.

'It's just that *this* can't be — I mean, you can't be seen like this. And I can't — ' she squatted down and studied her toes.

Meanwhile the sun rose and rose. I blinked at it. I thought I'd go blind with too much light. I blinked at her. I thought I saw her shimmer, like the rest of the ground now quickly heating up.

The shimmering figure stood up and undid her wrap. She cut it in two with her teeth. 'Here, Beena,' she said, handing me one of the pieces. 'Get dressed and let's get started.'

*

Can the tongue forget its thirst? And the stomach its hunger? No, Beenabe would tell me much later. But one could trick them to hide for a while, especially when there are more pressing occupations.

We waded through the skulls and bones, me lagging far behind. Impatiently she called out, 'Hurry up, hurry up,' but my legs were just learning how to carry me again. And the sun was drying my throat while my stomach reminded me of its existence. But I did not know how to say these in my head or how to call them out to the dot of brown way ahead of me. She had said we were to keep walking to the edge of this place, and that she'd know how to get us home from there. She had said we should think of only one thing, getting out of here. But my head was trying to find the words for thirst and hunger, and my feet were intent on not hurting the skulls and bones, especially the very few little ones. They were curled beside the big ones or the big ones were wrapped around the little ones. I nudged them with my toes and they moved as one. Maybe they had grown into each other. A big skull and a little skull in a mesh of bones.

Soon I was not even aware that I had lost Beenabe. I had stumbled upon a strangely beautiful creature. Set apart from the rest of the skeletons and mostly shaded by a boulder was a big skull with its full trunk wrapped gracefully around three little skulls of equal sizes and curved almost into a full circle. The creature, for it looked like only one creature, was mostly in shadow, looking safe, except the big skull. Facing the glare, it was so white and bright. I had to touch it.

My hand burned. I stared at the gaping mouth. It was pleading for me to move it out of the sun. It wanted to be safe like the little skulls so calm and contained in its circle of bones. I began to push the big skull into the shadow, but it snapped off its trunk and rolled away. The whole creature toppled down, dislodging all the little skulls out of their home.

I panicked. I heard me frantically whirring as I tried to catch all of the skulls and my brow itched, sending shivers to the rest of my face. I thought the whirring had grown wings and was struggling to fly out of me.

The big skull could not roll too far away. Something stopped it, no, not a bone but a smooth-looking mound not quite the colour of anything else around.

The whirring in my brow stopped too.

I picked up the little skulls, trying to make sense of each against the big one. I nudged the small mound that stopped it from rolling too far. It was smooth to the touch. I could not resist digging up all of it. I don't why, but when I had dug it out, I heard the right word in my head. *Hunger.* And the locust burrowed deeper into my brow.

It was curved. It was broken. It was cool to the touch.

I found myself looking at half a bowl. *Bowl.* The word rang inside my own skull and instinctively I touched my brow. All quiet up there. It had decided to stay small and snug and hidden.

I brought back my find into the shadow. But I could not put back the creature together again. All the little skulls would not fit into the circle of bones, as if that safe place had grown too small. And it was impossible to restore the big skull to its trunk.

I laid the skulls side by side, and then I began to dig again with my half a bowl. It felt like the most natural thing to do. I was looking for something, I didn't know what, but I could not find it. Once again I touched my brow instinctively but I could not feel it. My locust had burrowed too deeply. Small and snug and hidden.

Bowl. Hunger. Bowl. Hunger.

The words rang in my head, then found my mouth for the first time.

'B-bowl … h-hunger …' I spoke them to the skulls.

Silently they stared, as if waiting.

On my hand, the earth on the bowl seemed right, even if it was the wrong colour. Slowly I raised it to my mouth and began to feed.

☆

Someone was calling me, or was it really me?

'Beeee-naaaaaaa! Beeee-naaaaaaa!'

Urgent then desolate. I had heard such a cry before but not quite like this. And not quite here? Here all the colours were wrong. What was the right colour then?

The cry drew closer and I kept feeding. It was the most natural thing to do. My mouth remembered to chew slowly, to swallow slowly. 'So as not to choke, child, so as not to choke.' Who was whispering in my head? Then all went quiet. Earth rolled around in my mouth. Strange, this was not dry like what my tongue remembered and something was missing.

'Beena, couldn't you hear me, I've been looking — what — ?' She stared at me, at the bowl, at my mouth, then at the lined up skulls. Her face grew hard, eyes almost bulging. The sun burned, making a halo around her.

The blow was quick. The bowl flew out of my hands and I felt my cheek sting.

'You don't eat your kind.'

It was the most sorrowful voice that I would hear in my whole life.

*

It took us three more days to get out of there. The first day was for censure. The second was for walking around in circles. The third, for repair.

How could I explain to her I was not feeding on bones? And that the earth was not part of the dead? And that alive they would have partaken of my meal? Like once upon a time. How could I tell the old story? Like my face, memory was in patches and words were slow to come.

On the second day we walked with renewed purpose. After Beenabe named the place *Grave*.

'Not home, Beena. This is no longer your home. Home is over there,' she said, waving beyond her, then realising that beyond was nothing but more skulls and bones. Defiantly she addressed them, 'We'll get out of here,' and in an afterthought turned to me. 'You don't feed on a grave, Beena.'

I saw her swallow on the word 'feed', her throat hollowing, before walking ahead again. At first she did not own up to hunger or thirst, but she could not deny her exhaustion. She kept slipping to her knees.

'Bowl. Hunger,' I called out to her and for a while she stayed where she had fallen, as if my words had sat heavily on her shoulders. Then wearily, she got up and moved on.

Strange, but we kept walking away from and returning to

the creature that witnessed my feeding. The line of four skulls and the headless trunk kept pulling us back.

'You disturbed them, Beena, so they won't let us go.'

On the early morning of the third day, I woke up to Beenabe squatting before the skulls, not taking her eyes off them. She seemed to have sat there through the night.

'You disturbed their rest,' she said again but gently.

What did she know about the creature? I was the one who found it. And did I not try to put it back together again?

That morning I tried again. In the half-light they were only balls and sticks. The big ball on the top, the little ones inside the circle, but again the big ball rolled away and the third of the little balls would not fit.

'Break it then,' Beenabe murmured to herself, and once again I saw skulls and bones. She took the left out skull from me, forcing it back into the circle, snapping part of the ribs. Then she chipped the neck, so the head could rest on it though precariously.

Her face wore a look of pain, as if she were the one that broke. I stared. On the corner of her mouth, I saw bits of earth.

*

We finally left the last blessed stretch. But only after she had rubbed it all over my exposed parts. The earth cooled my face and I felt grateful. I had not known the burning sun for ten years.

'We're about to cross to the other side, so this must be done,' she said, rubbing more earth on me. I wanted to say, you had earth on your face too, close to your mouth. But I sensed that she'd hate to be found out.

My brow whirred with pleasure as each handful of earth touched my skin and settled there, for it did cling to me. The whirring continued, growing melodic. The sound surprised me. It had been so quiet up there for days.

After a while Beenabe surveyed her handiwork, turned my face this way and that, and said, 'You look better.'

I half understood. She wanted to cover my pale patches. She wanted to make me *one* colour.

Maybe I did feel better after her approval. After she had made me feel bad for the last three days. After all my transgressions, my inadequacies. Earlier she had studied my face and said, 'You are not beautiful.' Maybe she had thought I would not understand. But how could I miss her little shudder as she brought her face close to mine and touched it?

I sensed the same shudder when we finally reached the edge. I saw the skulls and bones resting beside each other in a long, long line. She cautioned me about the half-buried, twisted thing that also stretched in a long, long line. It had cut her, she said. It was dangerous. Then the shudder. Then she decided to make me look better.

I was not to forget this: I am not beautiful.

She was gentle with my face. She was careful not to disturb *that mark* on my brow. It whirred whenever her fingers got too close. It fascinated her, but she would never call it by its name. The word made her shudder too. Back home she had heard of locusts long ago and the hunger in their wake.

If only I could remember enough to tell the other story. Once upon a time locusts were sustenance. They kept themselves hidden because they smelled our hunger. Once upon a time locusts were silent.

It whirred even more loudly when her fingers grazed it. My brow itched in a pleasurable way.

'It's only one, but it sings like two,' she said in awe.

The whirring played three notes, sometimes all at the same time. It did harmonies, so alien to the pure rise and fall of single notes that Beenabe knew so well.

'Not like The Songs of my orange box,' she shook her head sorrowfully. I sensed that she was trying to be kind. She kept herself from saying her orange box was so beautiful and she missed it. She couldn't use the word *beautiful*. She had made me feel bad enough.

I was sensing too many things then, like little melodies in my skull.

We grew silent, staring at the other side. A different colour now, a different story. For miles and miles, brown under the unbearably hot sun. Then the horizon.

I made my move forward but was stopped. 'No, don't step there, those buried things are sharp,' she said, quickly lifting me over the line of skeletons to the other side. Her renewed strength surprised me. Then she put me down, saying, 'We're going home, Beena,' and almost smiled.

I felt a warm rush in my chest. My friend's eyes were soft. Her face was close to mine and this time she did not shudder.

'But tell me, Beena, how did you get that mark?'

'Peel your eyes off me
I am not beautiful
Peel your eyes off me
I am not the road'

☆

'I said, don't look behind you — ah, stubborn girl.' Beenabe's scolding returned as quickly as it had gone. 'Promise me you'll forget that place, we must forget that place. If anyone asks you, I was never there.'

How can she deny our story? Throughout that walk, she kept asking me to make promises against what we left behind. But sometimes when she told me about her home, she spoke about how she had spied the plains of black and white from the highest peak — 'But all that is past. Fix your eyes only on the line ahead, Beena.'

It shimmered in the heat, it undulated, or did I just imagine that? What was it really, a forever line or a stop line? Something for the eyes to follow endlessly or something to warn the feet that everything ended there? I had never seen the horizon before, until then.

'F-far … ' Another remembered word rolled in my mouth.

'Far, but we'll reach it,' she argued and after some hesitation added, 'We will get home. I walked all the way here from home, surely I can walk back.'

Each time we stopped to rest, Beenabe stretched her arms towards that long line, which we never seemed to reach. We were growing slower and my stomach insisted that it be acknowledged after ten years of denial. She could no longer stop me from bringing fistfuls of sand to my mouth. She looked at me with disgust, then with dismay, then with sadness. She who was used to scavenging and bringing home gifts for the table could find nothing among the sand or under stones, or between boulders and overhangs of rock. This desert was as mean as it was dry. Even our tongues had begun to shrivel. Soon all talk ceased. We would have been as silent as those skulls and bones, if not for the whirring in my brow.

It was this whirring that kept us moving. It whirred towards other sounds, or it led us towards them. It picked them up before we even heard it. A stray gust of wind, a rolling pebble, dust from a rock, and my brow itched in response, sometimes into full melody copying what it heard. It seemed to carry on a conversation with even a faraway sound and always our feet could not resist. We found ourselves walking to the source of the sound. Even our feet had been afflicted with the song of the locust.

'Meet me over there
My left foot says to my right
Where there still lies
A wee quiver of life'

*

From afar it was only a rock. Solitary, as if it had decided to shun its own kind. We had left the rugged terrain and were now walking through the flattest dryness, so the rock stood out like a bump in the horizon. Only a silent rock, but quickly my brow began to sing even before it itched. Beenabe and I stopped in our tracks and she looked back at me in wonder, for this was not the usual whirring. It confused me. It began as simultaneous notes, like a burst of harmonies that slowly tapered into three notes ultimately parting ways but all pushing our feet towards the rock. Soon the three notes became two, echoing the weary rise and fall of our soles. Then one of the notes grew faint, no, it had gone elsewhere. It had strayed from my brow to give voice to the rock, for it was also singing now, or was it? Just one note, like a subtle beat conversing with its abandoned pair in my brow.

Beenabe began to run towards the rock, but she was too weak, she kept falling. I lagged behind as usual. I had forgotten the possibilities of feet, their urgency to race each other. I saw her raised arm beckoning me forward, quickly, and jabbing at the air towards the bump in the horizon.

This time the two notes merged into one. My brow and that rock seemed to have melded. No more rise and fall, just the steady thudding of a single note. Ah, so familiar and so comforting. So unmistakable.

'Water!' Beenabe cried out. 'Over here, over here!'

But how could I follow her now? My knees had grown even weaker and someone was hushing me to sleep ... 'Riverrrr with a delicate roar, ocean with a ssshh ...' I lay down, lost in the steady dripping in my brow. It cooled me even as I curled up on hot sand. I am the vessel into which water drips. I will be full, I will be full and I'll grow up to be big and strong and good.

Big. Strong. Good. In my skull the words became the steady dripping. Who was speaking in there?

'Beeee-naaaaaaa! Beeee-naaaaaaa!'

Wrong name, wrong name, the voice in my head answered Beenabe's insistent call. I could hardly make out the speck of her, brown on vast brown. Quickly the whole world closed its eyes and the brown was swallowed by something cool and bright at the same time. It was round and curved, floating towards me. Like what I had dug up beside the creature that I could not put back together again. Like where the blessed earth had rested before it touched my mouth. How cool ... and whole and growing bigger, drawing closer. Bowl. Blue bowl about to cover me. *Blue.* How did I ever forget that?

Then it was brown. It was Beenabe shaking me, Beenabe finding her voice again. 'Beena, it's a hole, a cave — it's a cave with water — can't you hear it?'

What is the colour of water?

'We're saved, Beena, we're saved!'

What tongue unshrivels quickly with a rumour?

Beenabe could not stop talking and sobbing. It was one of her damp moments. 'Wake up, Beena, what's the matter with you? You can't do this to me, oh wake up, please! We have to go in there, there's water in there, can't you hear it, of course you can, you know this — and you — your — *it* must lead us there.'

Its one note dripped steadily and my brow stopped itching.

*

When I finally came to, it was dark. I thought night had fallen, but then I realised we were inside the cave. Beenabe had dragged me in, all the way from where I had fainted. I wondered how she found her strength. I could hear her scrambling around, scraping, digging with her hands, desperate for the rumour to be confirmed. My brow was silent now, but I knew in her head the dripping rang true, as loud as her hope.

Several times the world closed and opened its eyes, and each time I came to, I found her squatting beside me. She was not crying now. Like a stoic guard, she watched and waited for my brow to start singing again.

She had dragged me deeper into the cave and I felt like I had returned to my home of ten years. It was so dark, I could not even see my hands, and it was damp. Was it Beenabe's sweat, for she was holding me close again but with barely a shudder. She was fearless in her sleep. She mumbled stories that made sense only much later.

Not sweat. Indeed the ground was damp and so were the walls of the narrow cave. I was careful not to wake her as I groped my way in the dark, wanting to find the truth. Like Beenabe, I could not forget the rumour of water. Here was more proof. I brought my hand to my mouth. Indeed it was wet, but it tasted strange. Was this water? In response, my brow began singing. A soft dripping and somewhere deeper in the cave, its twin note.

'Beenabe ...' I whispered, not daring to disturb this rumour that had begun again.

She heard it too, she told me, first in her dream where she was not allowed to drink, much to her dismay. Whatever was in the brown barrel was not meant for drinking, her sisters said. In her dream, she was back home and severely scolded, for she had returned empty handed.

Dream. I had one too, I told her. The skulls and bones were alive, drinking from blue bowls. Five hundred thirsty mouths — where did that number come from? But I had no chance to ask. Beenabe waved my story away and finished telling her own. She said her sisters beat her, because she brought no gifts from her long trip. Too long for a girl, the eldest who should have stayed home to cook dinner. 'No drink for her then,' her sisters decided. So she woke up dying of thirst, she explained, to excuse her shameless licking of the walls when she found them damp.

'Water, Beena, water!'

This time it was I who guided her in the dark, led by the singing in my brow. We could tell the passage had begun to widen. We could no longer touch the walls and we could almost stand without knocking our heads on the roof. It was cooler here. No, it was cold. I held Beenabe close, half carrying her. Weak with thirst, she had stopped ranting.

Gradually the single note seemed to break into several notes again. Or were they echoes of one resonant dripping — of water on water? In our ears, the full realisation came. Somewhere here was a vessel of water gathering more water. Our tongues and throats ached in their dryness. Then our toes grew colder and wet. We took another step and our whole feet got wet, up to our ankles. A pool of water!

'Oh, Beena, water, water!' she cried, falling on her knees with a loud splash, then we were both drinking even if the water tasted strange, even if it was salty and we grew even thirstier — before another sound halted us. I touched my brow. Was it the one that sighed, for it was a sigh, wasn't it? And were those feet walking on water towards us? The sighing grew as loud as the beat of water on water. Beenabe clung to me, shaking. I could hear her teeth, then her screaming as a pair of cold, damp arms enfolded us, sighing into our ears.

My locust sighed in return.

*

Hush,' the woman sighed. I was certain it was a woman's voice. We were gathered into her damp sighing. She rocked us gently, as if her sighs were a lullaby, until Beenabe grew silent. Even the woman grew silent, but the single note kept on: water on water.

Then my head was getting wet. I reached out. Someone's cheeks were wet and they were not Beenabe's. I quickly withdrew my hand and dared not breathe when the woman spoke.

'Children?' In the dark the arms and hands were all over our bodies, trying to confirm a wish. 'Yes, children … ah, such a long time …'

'Who are you?' Beenabe's usual question even when she was distressed or terrified.

'Cho-choli,' the woman sobbed. 'Childless Cho-choli.'

The name rang through the cave like a plea and none of us could answer it. Her sobbing dragged itself up and down the cave and we were held tighter. We felt her bony arms, her clutching fingers. Then the single note of dripping water broke into a multitude of notes, of various pitches. It was her sobbing vibrating inside our skulls. Listening was painful, but we could not tell her to stop, not when she started telling us her story.

'Once upon a time my cheeks were dry, my eyes were dry. Once upon a time I had a husband and two children, a boy and a girl. Once upon a time their cheeks were dry, their eyes were dry …'

She went on and on. With those many 'once upon a times', perhaps Cho-choli's was a time so old, it was before anyone knew there was such a thing as time.

'But our well was not dry, yes, we had a well once upon a time. Our whole village could drink once upon a time, even our animals. It was green once upon a time — '

'Green! Tell us, what's that like?'

But Cho-choli seemed not to have heard Beenabe. 'Then the good men and women came to our village once upon a time. They came to tell us we had too much water and we were wasteful. We had to save water for the future. So they built pipes into our well and our water disappeared.'

Even my shoulders and arms were wet now, and so were Beenabe's. Cho-choli was bathing us in tears.

'Once upon a time the good men and women said they were the keepers of water. Once upon a time they said that our water was somewhere safe now for the future, and they promised to send us just enough water, so nothing will be wasted. So once upon a time there came barrels of water, which we had to share, but there was never enough and our well was completely dry. Then the barrels stopped coming. The good men and women forgot their promise. So our village began drying up, even the wombs of our women. But by that once upon a time, I already had two children, a boy and a girl, and they made me weep.'

Her tears dripped over our bodies into the pool where we stood — and it hit us. This was Cho-choli's water! Salty. Unstoppable in its dripping.

'Once upon a time as our village turned brown, our animals began to die, then our children. Do you understand what this means? So once upon a time all the husbands sought the good men and women to demand that they keep their promise. The mothers like me had to stay home to watch our children die. While once upon a time our husbands walked to the horizon and never came back. There were rumours of fires that sprouted along the way ... once upon a time.'

The cave was awash with sound and too much once upon a time. Each of her words became like dripping water. More notes added as her story went on and the locust in my brow began copying each note, playing it over and over. I thought my skull would split with this invasion. I had to stop her. My wet arms reached out again towards her face. I wanted to plug her mouth, her eyes, but quickly I shrank away. No eyes, no eyes!

'I wept, I wept them out
Find them in each sigh
I wept, I wept them out
Find them in each story'

*

We fled from the cave of the weeping woman, her stories pursuing us. How we ran, but we could not run away from the story of her green village once upon a time. Even if Beenabe said we should not speak about that cave ever again, I knew, like me, she was wondering about green.

What's green? Vaguely I remembered asking someone the same question long ago, but the present was a hot wave that washed it away. Outside it was as brown and dry as ever. Beenabe kept convincing herself that a story was never told, that it never happened. But how could she deny it when the saltiness remained in our mouths?

It took two days of walking for my brow to behave. It kept singing Cho-choli's story, as if to memorise it. So how could we deny it?

Beenabe refused to listen. She refused to walk with me. She was the one lagging behind now. She must stop to rest, she called out to me. But I saw from the corner of my eye that she was studying the brown sand, her brown wrap, her brown skin. On the second night as we lay together after a meal of sand, she finally asked me, 'What's green, Beena?'

I knotted my brow until it hurt, to remember. Nothing. Even my locust did not stir. We slept dreaming of green. We invented it. It became everything that was good once upon a time.

Green was anything we wanted it to be. Like dry cheeks and dry eyes or faces with eyes, or hot barley soup, or barley sprouting on blessed earth, or putting together again the creature that I had broken, or sleeping with sisters, or drinking not salty water, or walking past the horizon then home.

Or maybe it was a strange song that sneaked into our dreams. It began with a single note repeated at even pace, but it was unlike the earlier dripping. It went tap-tap-tap-tap continuously. It bewildered and blessed us. Beenabe dreamt of her sister's finger tapping the table before she served barley soup. I dreamt of something, was it a spoon, tapping the blue bowl, in a call for a walk after dinner. Soon the song became more than a tapping. Voices began singing over it, men's voices blending in a strange, beautiful way that we could not understand.

My brow stirred. I heard it mimic the song, which was faint and scratchy, with parts missing. We could not understand it, but the voices were so comforting. The song began again. Who were these singers? Maybe fathers sitting together after a meal? There was contentment in their voices and the final word sloped down, as if sighed out, but this was unlike the sighs in the cave. This had no pain. This was a sigh of good things. In my sleep I stroked my brow again and again.

We walked into a village that was like Beenabe's own, she said, but this one was empty. She held back her tears. She would refuse her own damp moments from then on. She would refuse to be like *that woman* in the cave. 'I don't want to lose my eyes, Beena.'

As we walked, the song kept playing in my brow and from somewhere, dragging our feet to its source. We visited each empty stone hut, tapping the song's rhythm on the door, wall, table, bed, as if calling for some revelation to be served to us. What is this place? We left our mark wherever we tapped, for the rhythm remained there, so when we entered the last hut, the whole deserted village seemed to be singing in harmony. The doors, the walls, the tables, the beds sang in different timbres but with that conspiratorial joy of gathering, of doing something together. 'Like when bodies bump into each other in a dance, our mother told us,' Beenabe whispered sadly. Once upon a time her village danced, she said, because the full rations still arrived and the sky was not yet brown.

Outside the last hut we stopped and kept our fingers from tapping, because the singing was in there, in there! It was loudest in there. We held our breaths before we pushed the door open. Those men's voices sound like they just had a full meal. Will they ask us to join them? Will they be kind? Will they offer us a meal?

But inside there was only a strange black and round animal spinning while its one arm scratched its face. The men are singing inside it, it's eaten the men! Beenabe and I backed away but we could not leave. We were held by this spinning thing. It kept singing to me, to us, then it sighed a real sigh, perhaps wanting to prove that not all sighs are unhappy. 'Aa-ahh — ' then the sigh went on, 'Ahh-ahh-ahh-ahh-ahh …' until a body rushed past us and quickly grabbed the animal's arm from its spinning face, and all singing stopped.

Beenabe and I backed off even further.

'It's not what you think, it's not what you think it is,' the tiny man or woman, for we could not tell, pleaded, hugging the animal to its chest and making ready to run away, but we were the first to reach the door and for a while we halted — the creature was scared of us!

It had long white strands sprouting from its head and shrunken face. This was hair that Beenabe's village knew before the ochre rain. The creature was very pale and smaller than me with gnarled, spindly limbs. It wore a brown wrap around its hips. Its pleading confused us.

'This isn't mine, I just found it, I burned mine once upon a time according to the law, I believe in purity too, no singing together, and each one has a definite place so no mixing up, I never did any mixing up, not then not now, I'm alone now and pure, so please don't tell on me to the masters, not to them please, not to them!'

'Who are you?' Trust Beenabe to ask the usual question.

'I'm going to burn this if you wish, just don't tell on me!' the creature slumped to his knees, cowering.

'Your animal ate the men.'

'Animal? Which animal — ah, this,' and here, the creature shook his head. 'No, no, it's a record — '

'How could you let it?'

'A record and a phonograph, can't you see?'

'The men are in there singing, eaten by your spinning animal — and what are they singing, huh?'

'They're singing about love, and they're in here and not in here,' he kept on. 'Because it's a record, you understand? It's not an animal but men singing about the love that you — that you and I, and anyone takes — '

'I don't take love,' Beenabe retorted. 'Because I've never been given it.'

The creature fell silent. Then it lifted the black thing and tenderly raised it to the light and it shimmered like a black sun. 'Look,' the creature said, 'It's the most beautiful thing, a most beautiful song by famous men once upon a time, but I kept it when I found it among the rubble, I couldn't burn it, because even now it keeps me believing that — that maybe — maybe we can give love as much as we take it. You see, that's what it's singing about, the taking and giving of love.'

'Humph, it's an animal singing a lie!' And she grabbed it from him.

'Please, please, be gentle with it, it's no animal, it's a record and it might break, so please — may I have it back?'

Beenabe did not break it, as I too feared. She stared at it, turned it this way and that, shook it, held it close to her ear.

'Why,' the creature whispered, perplexed, 'You've never seen a record before?'

Beenabe shook her head, then to my surprise carefully handed this thing back, murmuring, 'A lie but … it's beautiful. Can it — can it sing again?'

The creature finally smiled.

I loved copying it: simple stretching of the face, then parting of the lips.

☆

Was it a dream? Especially when it fed us a handful of dry black seeds, while making *the thing* that was no animal spin and spin again, as we listened? Then the door opened and another creature walked in with a jar.

'So you're alone?' Beenabe sneered.

Our host grew nervous but the newcomer walked calmly towards us and said, 'Our neighbour told me about you,' then offered us the jar. Water! Quickly Beenabe grabbed it and began to drink, but not beyond a sip. 'I know this taste,' she said, slowly licking her lips. 'Salty.'

'Of course,' the jar bearer said.

'Yes, I know this taste. The woman in the cave — '

A hand was waved as if to say, no more interruptions, then the creature turned to me. 'Now who are you, little one, and what happened to your face?'

How strange that it should call me 'little one' when it was smaller than I. Very long white hair wrapped around its neck to make sure it did not get in the way. It was as gnarled as the other creature, but of darker skin, and it was dressed like Beenabe. At least I could see its eyes, a shade that made me think of the bowl I found some days ago.

'She's Beena after my name Beenabe, because I found her,

and nothing happened to her face, I found it like that. So who are you?'

The creature frowned but answered anyway. 'Espra, and this is my husband Daninen.'

'And you said you're pure and don't do any mixing,' Beenabe snapped at Daninen. 'But your wife's a different colour!'

'Purity — hah! So, girl, they've filled your head with crazy ideas too?' Espra pushed Beenabe away and sat me down, undoing part of her wrap, which she dipped into the jug. Her movements were frugal and precise. She wiped my face, rubbing off the earth that Beenabe had applied. She stared at it. Daninen also stared. Thoughtfully they rubbed it between their fingers, then they stared at each other. I heard Daninen's cry of wonder as Espra took my face in her hands.

'Not sand, not dry ... this is blessed earth,' she whispered. 'Ah, Daninen, perhaps it can be green again.'

They confused me even more. I remembered the strange men intoning 'blessed' amid so many lights and the weeping woman's green village once upon a time, but all I could say was, 'G-green.'

'Ah, beautiful child, you have come to us with blessings,' Espra said and fed me more seeds.

Saying it was like smiling. 'Green.' My cheeks felt cool in her hands.

*

Trees are green. Trees are tall and proud and beautiful. Someone told me the same thing once upon a time.

As Espra wiped off the earth from my whole body and Daninen caught it with my brown wrap, they talked about trees. He had reluctantly set his silent animal aside and asked Beenabe not to touch it. Earlier she was hovering around it, frowning at it then at me. I sensed she resented the couple's censure or perhaps their awed affection towards me. Or Espra feeding me more. Or calling me 'beautiful.'

Was I? They gaped at my scarred body, while filling my ears with the rumour of trees. I was exposed and enthralled.

'You can't take off all of it. It's not earth, it's not blessed, it's skin — it's her, both light and dark. She *is* impure,' Beenabe said with such distaste, I felt I had lost a friend. 'And see that mark on her brow? Wait till it starts making funny sounds.'

My locust had been so quiet throughout this new encounter.

But Daninen was not listening. He was lost in his trees. 'Ah, Espra, how I miss the trees. Tell us, what trees grow in your village, Beena, and will you take us there?'

Beenabe laughed. 'What trees? Her village is gone.'

The couple looked at each other then at the gathered earth on my wrap. 'We lost our village too,' Daninen said. 'Before that, our trees. For the masters' houses, tables, beds, chairs, even their spoons. Ah, the hunger for trees, for the natural, for things pure. So the floods came and the cold, then this dryness and heat. I've lived this long for my eyes so they can see trees again. Take me to them, little foundling.'

'Daninen, Daninen!' Espra nudged him, suddenly agitated. 'The black — it won't come off.' She was eyeing me strangely now, as if she did not know whether to still like me.

'Told you,' Beenabe said.

Everyone stared. My nakedness had betrayed them. They examined my body with a disapproving sadness. Quickly I picked up my wrap and covered myself again, and all the earth I'd shed fell on the sand floor. They did not touch it now. I turned to Beenabe who had given me half of her clothing and had held me in her sleep, then I heard the first query from my mouth. 'W-why?'

Beenabe stared at her toes. 'Tell me about trees, Daninen.' For the first time she had our hosts' full attention.

It was a flat, thin thing, partly faded, which Daninen took from under the bed. There was something familiar about it, my eyes felt hot and watery.

'Come,' he beckoned to Beenabe who soon gathered with our hosts around this thing. 'This is the case of the record, of the song that you heard. This case protects the record from breaking. And on it, look, there's a picture of something that was once upon a time,' I heard him explain. I peeked over their heads to make sure I had seen right, that I had remembered right.

'Blue,' I said. 'Blue sky.'

'She's right, you know,' Espra said, pointing at the blue part of the picture. 'And these, Beenabe, these are trees. Blue sky, green trees, but they're not as blue and green as they really are, they're faded. And here, four men walking, also faded and torn, I think someone tore them out, but you can't miss them, they're walking in a line, one after another — '

'But I can only see their legs, their feet — how sure are you that they're men?' Beenabe countered the explanation.

'I just know that they're men, important men once upon a time.'

Beenabe examined the picture closely. 'Are they from the Kingdoms, or are they strays?' She frowned, trying to make sense of it all. 'Look, all these feet are wearing shoes, except one pair, so maybe he's a stray on bare feet, like us. Uhmm … walking to cross the border, like us. But they're not walking on desert — '

'No, they're crossing a road — that's a road,' Daninen

explained. 'A famous road called Abeeh, or Abah maybe, can't remember, such a long time ago.'

'Road — towards the horizon?' Beenabe asked.

'Beyond it,' Espra whispered.

'Where there are trees and the sky is not brown like here,' Daninen sighed.

'Where we can sing about love again,' Espra sighed too. 'Love that's green like the trees, blue like the sky, ah, Daninen, I miss them.'

Their circle was so intimate, it was not right to intrude, but my brow thought otherwise. It began to whirr, then sing. First the rhythmic tapping, then the chorus of singers assuring us — or warning us about how we take or give love? Then, the drawn-out sigh.

The circle broke up quickly and Daninen rushed to his animal — was it singing? But it was quiet and still. How come? He looked perplexed as he gingerly lifted the round, black thing, making sure not to touch its face.

'Told you. It's that mark singing on her brow!' Beenabe sniggered. 'It copies all sounds, so you better beware.'

Espra seemed even more unsure whether to like me or not, but Daninen was not looking at me now. He was slipping his singing animal into the picture of four men walking under the sky and the trees, towards the horizon.

*

Again the circle. Again I was outside it. I could hear their whispering. Then warmly our hosts hugged Beenabe goodbye but kept their distance from me. I did not miss their sad, curious glances. I wondered if Beenabe told them my story.

But did she not say to leave our tracks behind and not look back? The horizon was our only cause for walking. Walking to it was our only story.

We walked for five more days with Beenabe leading the way. I noticed her renewed energy, her purposeful strides, as if she knew where to go. We walked in patterns. I don't know how I came to notice them. Maybe because Beenabe had grown so distant and, feeling alone, I saw more. Sometimes we drew large circles with our tracks, then squares, then triangles that soon went around slim boulders of sand standing like frail sentinels. There was a smell about them. Beenabe sniffed the air and nodded to herself.

Nights were colder. Beenabe had stopped holding me in her sleep. On one of these nights, I saw her secretly munching the black seeds from Espra. I wanted to tell her she is beautiful, but my tongue could not yet wrap itself around the word.

'It's time to eat alone
The seeds are so few
It's time to sleep alone
The limbs are so tired'

*

He would have none of Beenabe's interruptions, even when she said that Daninen and Espra had sent us so he could lead us home. Fa-us was his name and we were sent to him to listen. At least, that was what he said.

We had walked into the tallest boulder as if it were porous and our bodies were air. In a circle of light, the old man sat. He looked like Daninen, but his hair was dark and we could see his eyes. They were the colour of the sky and the trees.

'Ah, children,' he greeted us. 'You will lead us out of this desert.'

Fa-us smelled like the boulders of sand, something both gritty and aromatic. It made us want to stand to attention and swoon at the same time. He raised a finger as if to warn us not to give in to the weakness of our knees. Then he beckoned to Beenabe who advanced in purposeful strides. She was sure this was her chance for deliverance. The old man wanted only her ear. I would never know what secrets he told her. I can only repeat what I heard for myself when my turn came.

First he rubbed my right ear, then the skin beneath it, murmuring, 'There was something here before, something written in blue ... uhmm ... but it's gone.'

'Blue ... gone ...' I murmured back, trying to remember what it was that had disappeared beneath my ear.

Then he whispered into it, his message slow. Each word seemed to be weighed first in his mouth that reeked with his perfume, before it was uttered.

'Child, remember this: we are held ransom by rumours. Rumours of water, colours, earth and trees. Even songs. All blessed rumours. Careful, you might think your life is also a rumour. You might think your life is not blessed. Lives are not rumours. They must be told openly. Lives are stories. They must be sung openly. Among all peoples, in small huts, in big halls, on the ground, up in the towers, for the old and the young, the able and the cripple. Plague them with songs, Child, not rumours. Rumours are not stories, are not songs. Rumours are in the air and we only catch and copy them, but songs are in the lungs and the throat even when they come up for air. And stories are lived in the bones.'

I imagined the bones where I came from as he ran his hands over my face, afflicting me with his perfume. My feet were firmly grounded but my knees grew even weaker and my cheeks felt warm. I thought they had grown smooth under his thorough hands. They sought every corner of my face. Then it dawned on me: his hands were his eyes. He was blind.

For a long time he touched my brow, with his lips. Then he smiled. 'Child, you will plague us, you will deliver us.'

My locust turned in my brow but silently.

'Go now. At last I can stop dreaming about you. At last I can wake up.'

Then the light went out and we were back among the thin boulders. We were still walking but not in patterns any more. Just one straight line now, as if our feet knew that we were on our way home.

There is beauty in certainty. She began to recognise the sand, the stones, even the rock that looked like a squatting woman, which she kissed. Her smile grew and so did mine. How I wished I could say the word, which I heard clearly in my head. How I wished I could call it out to her: *beautiful*.

Her arms opened to embrace her home, yes, it was out there, and I thought she'd lift herself into the air.

Ah, my beautiful Beenabe!

Then the brown sky lit up. She froze in her tracks. Lights, lights! We saw them, heard them in quick bursts. Lights, roaring lights! They afflicted our eyes, our ears, our tongues, our noses with their fire. Lights, blinding lights!

She began running towards them and I was so afraid.

*

In the fog my first thought was her village smells familiar.

After a while I saw the black bodies.

A charred man was dragging himself on one leg. I wanted to ask him a question, but I could not open my mouth.

Behind him was a woman with arms curved like a cradle, but it was empty.

They disappeared into the fog.

I saw a few more, walking silently as if the lights had burned out their voices. My brow itched like my throat as my lungs heaved and I remembered a name. 'Abarama, Abarama,' I heard myself whisper. Something was happening to my eyes and cheeks. It was so familiar.

'Fathers who do not speak
Make me speak
Mothers who do not weep
Make me weep'

SINGING

♪

Three years later

♪

The stars were out. I wondered if I would ever recover from the shock of seeing them again. The first time they began to appear to light my journey, I heard the percussion of spoons but could not remember more. Always I heard songs, names, little refrains from the past, quickly driven away by flashes of light and a girl opening her arms to a conflagration.

I missed Beenabe, sometimes unbearably. In my head, she was my only story, my only sorrow. How could I know that all my old sorrows had been collected into her story? How could I know I was missing the old sorrows even more?

My face, except for my brow, was almost clear by then. Tears had washed away my scars. After I left Beenabe's burning village, I went back to Cho-choli's cave to weep with her for three long years. She taught me the rudiments of sighing and the rhythms of the tide in the eyes. She had wept them out, leaving empty sockets, but not the memory of weeping. Or the memory of those once upon a times from her own time, her mother's, her grandmother's and all the women who had wept out their stories about the drying up of water and the earth, of trees and daily fare, even of colours. Because all these blessings were wasted or taken far away. Because of stupid wars. Because of great fires that fell from the sky or sprouted from the earth and dried up their insides, their wombs then their hearts. That dried up even the love among lovers.

Cho-choli taught me how to think as deeply as her pool of tears and how to speak with words that could rise to the sky. Then she taught me how to query all thought and speech, even her stories, as we wept and drank our tears, as we flooded the cave. We had to keep moving to higher ground, so we would not drown, and we kept on asking why. The creature in my brow chastised me silently, singing ditties against my indulgence, but only in my head. At first it sang aloud songs of commiseration and comfort for the weepers, then it grew tired and bored. It turned endlessly in my brow, urging me to leave. Cho-choli wound a piece of cloth around it before she let me go amid her sorrowful protests. She said the locust could betray me.

So in this strange place, stars again. Stars as early as dusk, when the trading began in whispers. An old man had his mouth close to the ear of a younger one who was as tall as the remaining wall. The old man had to tiptoe on a pile of rubble to reach him. Both were hiding in a corner cramped with debris, but I could tell the tall one was watching me throughout the transaction. He slipped two handfuls of seeds into the old man's bag in exchange for what looked like a shining stone. He took this out from the bag himself, because the old man had no hands.

They traded with seriousness and avoided each other's eyes. No one smiled. My face missed the gesture. It was a cold place on a cold dusk. The traders hugged brown blankets around themselves. Everywhere the ritual was silent: mouth to ear then the furtive exchange. Brown beads for a jug of water. Two earthen bowls for seeds. The woman who received the jug took one small sip, then stopped guiltily before the second. Quickly the jug disappeared under her blanket, as she did behind the rubble. The one who gave up her bowls took longer to slip away as if she wanted to change her mind. I saw how she had fondled the bowls tenderly, perhaps her last crockery. Where to serve this handful of seeds now.

I barely caught sight of a face. They slipped in and out of the ruins quickly, silently. I had stopped for shelter here last night and like ghosts they had begun coming and leaving in haste before my second night. Hands clutched old possessions, then the measly purchase. I did not know if they spoke my tongue.

Behind the wreckage, I eavesdropped. I caught the occasional click of a tongue, the hiss between teeth. I edged close to the remains of a window. I made out a line of shadows. Men or women? All heads were cleanly shaven and linked by mouth to ear and mouth to ear as if they were trading in rumours, or a chain of secrets. I heard a cry, instantly hushed, but it echoed. Quickly I pressed my bandaged brow. Hush, I whispered in my own head. It's not polite to mimic despair, not polite to spy. But my brow did not even stir. I abandoned the window. Perhaps I will sleep here for one more night. But another cry, louder this time, brought me back to my feet. The shadows were now rocking themselves, until the cry faded to a whimper. What was this transaction? For a while, I imagined their only business was silence.

Then I lost them. Someone had covered the window with his back. It was the tall man trading earlier. I heard him clear his throat and that was all. I heard no more, I saw no more. Until the ruins began to sing.

'Lest we forget —
There is only one story
There is only one song
That we take home'

♪

A song that assaults everything in its way often settles in the bones. You believe it, because you have no choice. This was what I thought of the clean rise and fall of words, which I readily understood. So these traders speak my tongue? Had I come home to my own kind?

Underneath my feet, the ravaged floor vibrated. The song was rising from its pores, or so I felt. I tightened the bandage around my head. My brow was gearing up for a response, which I could not allow. Then I heard them.

'One story. One song.' A meek echo from the line of shadows, but not whispered together. Each had to say it alone with that careful enunciation reserved for wishes.

I peeked again. The tall man had left the window and was breaking up the chain of shadows with what looked like a whip. He was doing it wordlessly and the shadows were rushing out of the ruins also mutely. The silent violence was unnerving. My feet almost rushed out with them as if the whip were also after me. Then I saw the culprit: a box the size of the man's head. Blue! My heart skipped a beat. I sensed older songs. *No one should look … No one should walk …* I closed my eyes, I stopped my feet.

When the blue box had exhausted its singing, I sneaked out of the ruins. I made sure even my blanket was securely gathered into silence.

♪

For a while I was torn between contemplating the sky and following the chain of shadows, for they had sneaked back into the ruins. I ended up stumbling after them. I had to know what passed between mouth and ear, my brow had to know. This lone companion in my wanderings always led me to its intimate occupation: sound or its possibility, even its absence. Always it wanted to hear why or why not. These days, it listened more than it sang and it argued with me. It even mocked me.

Soon I found myself descending into a hole. I'm used to this, I told myself, but still my throat and lungs longed for more air, more air. Somewhere below, I heard the clicking of tongues and the hiss between teeth moving further away. Then the heavy footsteps above, very close to my hand hanging on to a ledge for support with little confidence. Ah, I had been out in the open for too long, my brow mocked me.

Someone up there was pacing, trying to decide whether to descend or not. I held my breath. The pacing multiplied. More footsteps had arrived, slow and heavier, as if this newcomer were weighed down by some burden. Just then, my grip on the ledge began slipping. Instinctively my other hand reached out to steady myself. It was inevitable. The blanket I was clutching fell and quickly I followed.

Sound saves as much as it betrays. Up there the newcomer was just setting down the burden too loudly, so my fall was disguised. Then I heard the pouring of seeds, quite unmistakable, followed by water. It had to be water gurgling into smaller jugs. What else could it be? Before I would reach the Five Kingdoms, I would know only basic fare. It would not occur to me that there was something else beyond this.

When my eyes had adjusted to the pitch black, I found myself surrounded by tunnels. No, more like doorways with intricate awnings. They threw patterns on the tunnel walls after the first glimmer of light from one of the doorways. I did not enter here, though, even when the light grew warm and welcoming.

Instead I crept into the next tunnel, for I realised it had cracks that I could peek through. The tunnel walls felt uneven, shifting slightly under my hands, which I quickly withdrew.

I saw them again, their shaven heads still, their eyes closed. Before them was a blue vial of light which looked familiar. Light and shadow played on the finely formed skulls. All beautiful, features exquisitely sculpted. My breast felt tight, it hurt to breathe. I imagined Beenabe among them.

It was not long before the whispers grew audible. There were six of them, trading in rumours. *Only* rumours. For how else could they have known this much in a landscape of mostly drab brown?

'Red,' the first mouth whispered to the second ear, who whispered back, 'Red flowers,' and then passed on the next colour to the third in line: 'Orange.'

'Orange birds,' the third mouth whispered back and, to the fourth, passed on: 'Blue.'

'Blue sky,' the fourth mouth whispered back and, to the fifth, passed on: 'Yellow.'

'Yellow fields,' the fifth mouth whispered back and, to the last, whispered: 'Green.'

All grew silent.

'Green trees,' someone eventually answered and all opened their eyes. Fearfully they looked around. Then 'steal' and 'dreams' floated in the air like disembodied words as if no mouth had spoken them. Then the light was discreetly extinguished.

My brow kept listening to what remained unsaid.

♪

When the footsteps began descending, the conjurers urgently

resumed trade. Their rumours rushed into stories all whispered in song. Orange birds began to fly through blue skies and over red flowers and yellow fields lined with green trees. In the dark I had a lesson in colour until the stories came to a halt. A short man, but heavily built, had just descended. He slapped the most earnest storyteller into silence. Someone punched him in turn. It was the man as tall as the wall who then began soothing the slapped cheek with some oil from a pouch. I caught a whiff of something both gritty and aromatic but only momentarily.

The other whisperers kept their heads bowed. They could not bear to look at the injured one. When the men arrived, she had been conjuring the blue ocean and how they could sail away on it.

The men had their own vial of light. It flickered and cast shadows. The tall one looked even taller, even if he was on his knees. He brought the light close to the bruised cheek. A young girl, or maybe a boy? He shut the victim's eyes while he ministered to the bruise, as if he could not bear the injured stare. I was perplexed. Such kindness from someone who held the whip earlier? He kept clearing his throat as he ran his fingers over the bruise again and again, trying to erase it, I thought. The other man looked on but kept his hands to himself. It was he who would later herd the youths back to the ruins above, while his tall companion lit the way.

♪

I woke up to noise and the first voices that refused to whisper. I thought they were speaking another tongue. My brow demanded I close my eyes to hear better. Soon I tuned in to the words, their strange rhythm.

'Give me that, Gurimar — I have the pouch.'

'But I have the two hands.'

'Of course. Why do you always treat me like a cripple?'

Laughter from both as if the question was a very funny joke. Then again the noise, like someone pounding or breaking something. I peeked through one of the holes, but the next tunnel was empty except for what seemed to be mounds of rubbish. I realised my tunnel wall was also a mound of rubbish that rose to the roof.

'Oh, look, Hara-haran, so many of them. Aren't we lucky?'

'Lucky, yeah, they're old but still with drops in them — go on, do the pouring with those *two* hands,' she sniggered.

I heard no pouring, only something dragging around. I shut my eyes to hear better. I had woken up to what looked like rubbish everywhere, visible through bits of light streaming from holes in the roof. The uneven tunnel walls were piles of little boxes burnt black. There were also vials and what looked like more burnt rubble. Last night's intricate awnings were nothing but ancient cobwebs. I had slept in an underground dump.

'Stop playing with them, Hara-haran.'

'I think they're pretty.'

Slowly I crawled towards the voices, avoiding the shafts of light, keeping myself hidden. Among the rubbish were a boy and a girl and a stack of the boxes, each fist-sized. She was trying to balance them precariously with one hand, which was all she had. Then she dragged herself around her handiwork, admiring it. Her lower limbs ended at her knees.

'See, a tower, Gurimar. Oh, I'm smart.'

'C'mon, let's finish up,' the boy said, scavenging among the rubbish, picking up a box or a vial, shaking it against his ear or breaking it with a twisted metal staff. 'Might be more here.'

Both wore long shirts, torn and almost as black as the rubbish. Hair stuck out from their scalps like petrified clumps.

'See this, Hara-haran? Still half full — someone must have dropped it.'

'Still smells too, don't you think?'

'Uhmm ... hardly. But looks okay.'

It was the vial of light of the whisperers. Gone black as if it had burnt out. The boy had broken it and was pouring its remaining oil into the girl's pouch. Their faces were radiant. It was the most precious find of the day.

♪

'Are you spying on us?' The boy was ready to deliver a blow with his staff. I did not hear him creep behind me until it was too late.

'Who are you and who sent you?' The girl had pulled the blanket off me and was wrapping it around herself. 'Isn't she an ugly thing?' she taunted me, eyes on my scarred arms and legs.

'Answer her,' the boy demanded. He was hopping around me now, staff on the ready. He had only one leg.

'Answer, quick!' The girl pounded the ground with a fist to egg him on. Her eyes told me she wanted the staff to land.

The children were a bold and angry pair, perhaps both my height if they had all of their limbs. 'Whose spy are you?' they asked.

'Beena, I'm Beena, and no one sent me.'

'What kind of a name is that?' the boy asked.

'Because I'm from somewhere else, but I'm not spying.'

This angered the girl even more. Her fist was making a dent on the ground. She pointed at my bandaged brow. 'And what's that? What do you have under that brown thing?' To my surprise, it had begun to whirr. It had been sulking quietly for a year. No songs at all, just mocking asides silently planted into my thoughts. I had missed even the itching.

'You're hiding something.' The boy stepped back, dragging the girl with him. Both were suddenly unsure when the whirring became a tune, which I had never heard before. 'What is it?'

What could I say?

As the tune grew into a full song, the children moved away, whispering arguments into each other's ear. They could not agree. I thought they would hit each other with those waving fists.

It was the girl who calmed down first. She dragged herself away from the boy, face buried on her one hand. Then she asked me, 'How come you know *that* song?'

The boy protested against his sister's betrayal. They had promised each other not to tell anyone about *that* song. His mouth remained tightly shut as if he would never speak again.

♪

It was too early for a lullaby but my brow rocked us to sleep.

'You want a story?
But with no silences
You want a song?
To sing the silences'

Each query dangled in the air, as if the song had already ended or as if silence were indeed being sung before the next line. Maybe lullabies have gaps that sing our dreams. Before my eyes shut, I saw the girl snuggle close to her brother with my blanket.

'Mother sang that beautifully, remember?'
Silence from Gurimar
'Did she sing the silences too, before she left?'
Her questions hung in the air. He was sleeping.

♪

'No pushing, no pushing, let's get on with it — listen now, I'm warning you!'

The order could not subdue the din above, which woke the children first. They went wild. 'Ration time, ration time!' They raced each other up the hole without even a look at me.

It was pitch dark again. My third night now and I had lost my blanket, Cho-choli's going away gift offered with caution about the chill of faraway places. I was shivering, exposed to the cold and later to the colder stares. I felt my scars. I am not beautiful. So was it safe to go up? My thirst and hunger answered. I need the rations. Here the sand was not the fine sort that was kind to the stomach. Anyway there was the kindness of the dark. I could keep to the shadows.

A long line of noisy shadows bisected the desert, pestered by the strays trying to push into the line. All were waving about some flickering light. These were my first visions from a smashed window. And within the ruins, sacks, barrels and jars were being checked by silent men, two of whom I recognised. The tall man and his shorter lackey were dressed in the usual drab brown, without the cumbersome blankets but with their own lights around their necks. The little vial.

Suddenly the lackey began beating one of the sacks, cursing under his breath. The sack was moving and crying out. By the time it was thrown out of the ruins, its knot had come undone, and among the spilled seeds I saw the old man who had paid with a shining stone the night before. The tall man was quickly on his knees to soothe the bloody head with oil from one of the jars, clearing his throat all the while.

Ah, that gritty and aromatic smell. Of course, Fa-us's perfumed hands! I remembered the scent and felt the same weakening of my knees while wishing to stand to attention. I leaned out of the window, filling my lungs with the night air and my eyes with the stars, trying to restore balance. But even out there, the smell wafted from a long, long line of flickering lights. They were like agitated stars jostling each other at ground level. I saw the old man crawl out of the sack and disappear among the crowd.

'No pushing, no pushing, get to the end of the line, you, and you too!' the tall man ordered the strays, cracking his whip on the wall. A shining stone hung from his neck. A deep blue stone that burned brighter than the light beside it. Ah, the stone from the old man without hands; it was held together by a necklace of brown seeds. Food and fire, I thought.

The strays were still trying to push in, arguing under their breaths.

'Did you hear me? Back, back — to the end of the line! Jump the queue and you won't get anything tonight — I'm warning you.'

Tonight? How will they ever get to the end of that line?

It would take at least six nights, only the nights, to finish the task. The days were for sleeping, for hiding. Each time the sun appeared, all crept under their blankets and slept. The day brought a sharper chill around my heart. It was like seeing a line of brown corpses stretched towards the horizon. Indeed the dark was kinder.

♪

Scalps without hair, sockets without eyes, shoulders or elbows without arms, arms without hands, knees without legs, even a face missing both ears. Later I would hear it was because of the fires that still sprouted from the earth, though they had been planted there once upon a time. Everywhere I looked no body was complete. Their vials of light exposed them, but the scent from the burning oils softened this betrayal. I even felt at ease with my own scars, but not with my shock at this wretchedness, which was soon jostled out of me. In the gritty and aromatic chill, I was dragged by the strays towards the end of the line, until about halfway through when a hand grabbed my arm and pulled me under a blanket. I was now in the line. Someone grumbled then yelped in pain. Gurimar had jabbed the protestor with an elbow.

'Don't get smug now,' he whispered to me. 'You're here only because of *that* song. You'll tell us how you know it but not here.'

I found myself with the two children under the blanket. Quickly Hara-haran began whispering instructions. 'Get ready. I go first, then Gurimar. You'll pick up the trick, it works,' then she jumped on my shoulders, wrapping the remains of her legs around my neck. I nearly fell over.

She arranged the blanket so we seemed like one body in the line. Only her face and arms were exposed. 'Move,' she urged me forward. 'And don't dare show yourself.'

'Don't dare show myself?' a male voice behind us protested. 'I've as much right to be here in this forsaken place — '

'Shut up, I'm talking to myself!' Hara-haran snapped, then in a change of heart, took on a comradely tone. 'See the chief over there, waving his whip and preening with that blue stone on his neck. As if we don't know where he got it. I'd love to bash him.' She never minced her words. 'Trading our rations for a frippery, that vain animal!'

'Like selling our souls to ourselves,' the man agreed.

I now understood the trading last night. 'I saw,' I whispered but could not say more. Gurimar's hand had pressed on my mouth. I could smell the children's hate. My head hurt with it.

'There was some trading in colours too. Underground, I heard.' The man kept up the comradely lull.

'Trading in stupid dreams!' Hara-haran spat out. 'Colours — hah!'

'We refuse to dream only in brown, we're human too.'

'*We*? Why — were you among those dreamers?'

'I mean — I know that kind of trade is a crime but — '

'What crime?' Hara-haran's hand dug hard on my shoulder. 'What's more criminal than selling to us what's rightfully ours?'

Strangely, she was so light. Or was it because I was strong, made strong by too many journeys?

After a while, the man whispered. 'Those stories of colour can keep anyone from despair, you know.'

'What's colour?' Hara-haran muttered to herself. I sensed a note of longing.

'Colours are ... I wish — '

'Shut up,' she snapped, to shut her own longing.

But he continued. 'Hard to be a stray with no village.'

'Speak for yourself. I had a village.'

'Last night, my wife lost her last crockery.'

'I'd just love to bash him.'

Her breath warmed the top of my crown where the scars were fading.

♪

'Lest we forget —
There is only one story
There is only one song
That we take home'

It had to be played before the rations, and the dutiful crowd echoed, 'One story. One song.' But there was no conviction in their response.

Way ahead the tall man waved his whip about. 'I did not hear you,' he called out.

This time, the crowd chanted in earnest. 'One story! One song!'

'Good, good. Now listen, before we start, you have to be honest and true. Or you don't get anything.'

Agitated murmur down the line, then the fearful shifting.

'We all know that among you are six strays who have betrayed us. Last night, they attempted to walk to the border.'

The silence was a more cutting chill. Even breaths were halted.

'You must purge them from your kind. They've betrayed you from getting your rations promptly tonight, and — you might not even get them.'

It did not take long before the beautiful youths with shaven heads were pushed out of the line. Still chained together by mouth to ear and mouth to ear, passing on rumours of salvation. Quickly they were taken away by the short man who had slapped one of them.

Anger and guilt ebbed and flowed through the line. The lights burned brighter and grit rose from their oils.

'The trees,' Hara-haran sighed towards the disappearing youths.

'Beautiful and green,' someone in the line sighed with her.

From my brow, I heard again the whisperers trading in colours and how they halted fearfully in 'green.' I heard Daninen's rumour of trees: 'Ah, the hunger for trees, for the natural, for things pure.' Then a faraway voice telling stories about someone dancing with beautiful ladies who danced like trees with the scent of wind behind their ears. My confusion hurt.

♪

Green was anything we wanted it to be. Like dry cheeks and dry eyes or faces with eyes, or hot barley soup, or barley sprouting on blessed earth. I remembered how Beenabe and I dreamt up the colour together to ease our thirst and hunger. How was I to know that dreams could be stolen and changed, so we wake to a nightmare?

Inige would later tell about the nightmare. She was one of the six whisperers who were to be smuggled through the border after they were thrown out of the ration line. They were not even meant to be in the line. They were only walking past, away from their village that was warned about a purge, a fire. They were arrested on their walk. They had transgressed; no strays can walk to the border.

Later Inige would escape to tell her own story about green. She was a green tree. 'Green' for nubile. 'Green tree' for nubile youth. Green for breasts just beginning to bud and wombs waking up to a cycle. Green for voices just beginning to break. Green was pure and clean. And innocent. Beyond the border, green was anything they wanted it to be.

Inige was 'a good, green tree.' She could fetch a good price.

A sack of seeds. Two barrels of water. A jug of oil. It was a shame that her cheek was bruised. Two jugs of oil would have been a better deal.

♪

On the third day of queuing, we were warned to play our best by the sounds around us. There were censures, feeble pleas.

'Where's your mother?'

'She left,' a small voice answered further up.

'Your father — ?'

'Left too — please — '

'Where to? The border?'

'No, sir, no — they're — they're — maybe dead.'

An intake of breath somewhere, then the shuffling of feet, the restless hands rubbing empty pouches and jugs.

'You know the rule,' the blue stone man cleared his throat loudly as if he were hurting there. 'Rations are no child's play — what's the rule again?'

'*No wasting, no children in the line,*' the hungry mouths were quick to answer then scold the boy who had come alone with his empty pouch and jug. Suddenly I understood 'the trick' planned by Gurimar and Hara-haran. I braced my shoulders. When our turn comes, these children will stand tall and grown up on my back.

'Please, sir — just a little bit — '

Then, I realised that there were hardly any children in the line. How was I to know that there were hardly any children anywhere in that wretched place and time? Had Cho-choli not spoken about the inner dry?

'Get away, you! You're holding us up!' the waiting mouths

spat out their despair. Most of the women's wombs were dry, most of the men's seeds were dry. How dare this boy remind them, this painfully?

'Just a pinch of seeds, sir, just a sip of water, just to wet my mouth — '

'Sorry, little one, we must be fair.' The voice made sure it was thick with kindness and woe. 'How sad if I gave in to your wish — uhm — the rule's for all of us — uhm — no one is less or more in anyone's eyes, we're all equal — uhm — just as these seeds are equal in size and shape — uhm — so we can have a just rationing.' Then he fondled the blue stone thoughtfully before he announced with aplomb: '*Symmetry. Equality. Justice.* Yes, yes, we honour them, we dwell in them.'

Those words. Where have I heard them before? My brow lined them up in my ear. My mouth tested them. So grand and difficult, so dry.

♪

'I'm just doing — uhm — my job. Just me — uhm — care for you and pass on the care and blessings of the Five Kingdoms to you. They have not forgotten you. And just me — uhm — will never forget you. See what I brought? These sacks of very good seeds, these barrels of sweet water, these jars of fragrant oil. Our oil of grace for cooking, for light, for salving wounds and aches — all these for free, just-me-uhm will see to it, so we must be grateful!'

'Just-me-uhm, Just-me-uhm, Just-me-uhm!' Hara-haran chanted and giggled under her breath.

Someone tried to hush her. 'Want to be thrown out of the line too?'

'*Just-me-uhm*. That's how we call him, with those noises in his throat.'

'I'm sorry about these — uhm — bad turns of fate. But that child had to go, those whisperers had to go. I must — uhm — we must expel the impurities that are bad for the stomach and worse for the soul. We must uphold purity especially in this ration line, which preserves us all. We stick to the rules and the rules are for all. No bad or wrong seeds in the line. Don't the Five Kingdoms feed you only good seeds?'

I was getting more confused. It was very hard to follow Just-me-uhm's big words, but the way they disturbed the air was enough to chill everyone into silence, except the children.

Hara-haran was again digging her hand on my back. 'He always has to sound good and kind — just-me is good, just-me is kind — hah!'

Just-me-uhm. A beautiful man with lots of hair. Oiled and golden, more so with the light around his neck. He was heads taller than everyone else. He took regular trips through the border. He was well fed, well groomed, well trained by his father. He was a bastard of the Five Kingdoms. His mother was a 'green tree' favoured by the Minister of Mouths who kept her, but only until the boy was an uncomplicated joy. Just-me-uhm was always grateful for his mother's fate. Look at who I am now? So he smuggled green trees across the border. He was doing them a favour. When will they ever understand, these stupid wretches?

I learned more about him from the rumours down the line. He fancied himself as the Minister's mouth outside the Kingdoms. When he was barely five years old, he memorised the Kingdoms' Missions. They were sung daily by his father, then relayed through all the little boxes that were also rationed once. He missed the Missions, they were out of fashion now, and he missed their martial tunes. Nowadays singing them was thought unwise. Just-me-uhm suspected, not without some pain, that his father's singing embarrassed the other ministers. He had not seen him since he was six. Not wishing to complicate his vocal duties, the Minister of Mouths expelled his bastard son from the Kingdoms. But he continued to look out for his interests and assigned him the task of rationing outside the border.

I would learn more about him much later — how Just-me-uhm missed the Missions, which he had memorised only in his head. He could not sing; he was tone-deaf. His father never recovered from this tragedy thus sent him and his mother away. That was the true story: a bad turn of fate. But Just-me-uhm remained loyal, always apologetically clearing his throat whenever bad turns happened. He never forgot the Missions and their comforting logic. He sang it in his head. It assured him that he belonged to his father.

We will protect you
We will care for you
We will think for you
We will act for you
We will be you
What is yours will be ours
Rejoice, rejoice! You are ours
You are part of Kingdom building

♪

It was our turn. Finally I saw how truly beautiful he was. His oiled curls glinted. And how smooth his cheeks. How like a boy in the earnest conduct of his duty. I was grateful for the holes in my blanket. I watched his eyes shimmer like his blue stone and even grow soft as Hara-haran played her act to perfection on my shoulders.

'Rejoice, rejoice, my heart says to you, good sir. Your caring made me yours. My last limb is yours, if it pleases you, and so is my head, and so is my heart.'

Later the children would tell me about how they heard the Kingdoms' Missions from their father who heard them from his father, who heard them from his father who heard them from a little box once upon a time.

Evoking the Missions at ration time was the ultimate trick. It never failed. The man's eyes shimmered even more. 'Good woman, I accept your joy, your limb, your head, your heart. How well you know the wishes of the Five Kingdoms — open your pouch and receive their blessings.'

She did and seeds poured into it. And water gurgled into her jug. And oil slid smoothly into another pouch. She came prepared and her tongue was even smoother.

'Rejoice, good sir. You are part of Kingdom building, you are truly a Kingdom builder and I am your servant.'

Another handful of seeds, another gurgle of water. All saved for later. The children chose to remain hungry to feed a more pressing need.

In an afterthought, the Kingdom builder added a few more drops of oil. Hara-haran almost kissed his hand, which he quickly hid in his pocket. He made sure he did not touch and was not touched publicly by the strays. Usually the other men did the rationing, and the later duties, which I was to discover soon. But he gave the orders. He believed that he was indeed 'Just.' He gave rewards where rewards were due.

A little later, after we had pushed our way back into the line for a second act on my back, Gurimar had his share of rewards.

Rewards must be equally shared. Must be *reciprocal.* It was a big word that I would later hear in the Five Kingdoms. That I would see at work on the sixth day of the rations. The night before was freezing and afflicted with a new smell so foul, we had to plug our noses. The remaining hungry mouths whispered rumours that made the air whine beyond consolation. Distraught mouth to distraught ear and on it went, until the fresh rumour reached my own shocked ears. It was a rumour secretly blessed by the Five Kingdoms. A rumour that unfolded into a true story when the sun rose on the sixth day and the crowd crawled under the blankets to hide their limbs yet unclaimed by the great fires. When the silent men left the ruins to pick out the healthiest in the line.

Rewards were reciprocal. Rewards were harvested under the blankets. Eyes here, last good leg there, maybe that hand with the ring. And deeper down, more precious parts that could be traded across the border.

What is yours will be ours.

The smell of fear rose with the sun. Among the men scavenging for a heart, a liver, a kidney, my brow decided to betray me. The singing was out now for all to hear. No lullaby could have been more plaintive.

'What is mine will be yours
My child rejoice, rejoice
So the heart of the father
Sings to this sleeping thing'

♪

Running. I never knew that feet could ache so and that the breast could run out of air, even if there was so much of it around. The wind had begun to rise as we rolled down the steep dunes and burrowed our bodies into the sand. We kept so still, until, fearing a sandstorm, the men from the ruins abandoned pursuit. We were saved but not the jugs of water that broke in our haste.

'Why did you have to sing? Why did you not keep still? Why did you betray us?'

I thought Hara-haran's breast would burst with her anger. To her, all that mattered was that I sang, not what I sang. She was rubbing her only hand that had caught one of the men's eyes. It was fondled for texture and weight — but this is a child's! — until Gurimar hit him and pushed her onto my shoulders. Then we did not stop running.

'She's hiding songs under that bandage, hiding one of those boxes!'

'We'll make her pay, we'll make her tell us why.'

'Us? What will she tell that you don't already know, Gurimar?'

'What do you mean?'

'Mother's song — and yours? You, her favoured one, of course. You who never tell the truth about her, you never answer when I ask, and I ask and ask, every day I ask, but you shut your mouth and turn away.' She was screaming now. 'You've kept silent since you came home without her, and she never came home, she never came home, and you've never told me why.' Her lone fist pounded the sand, which had begun to whirl into eddies.

Gurimar's mouth remained a taut line.

'She took you walking, only you, because you could. And she never came home as she promised. So I'll find out the truth for myself, I'll force this ugly girl to tell me,' and she lunged forward, grabbing my bandage off.

It whirred. It preened. It fluttered its wings.

Shock, then screams. 'The plague, the plague!' They began to run again, from me.

So soon, the wind drowned the screaming. It picked up sand and wind became sand. So soon, the children disappeared in the storm but not their revulsion. It trailed the wind, it whirled about. The plague, the plague!

Beenabe, oh Beenabe, I am not beautiful.

The whole desert rose. It cut my skin, it opened scars, it cut my eyes. At least there was a reason to cry.

'So soon the loss
Before the love
So soon before
The silence broke'

♪

When the desert settled, I saw that it had become another place. The wind had rearranged the earth. Maybe Beenabe was right when she said that the old stories never happened. I was alone again and walking. I promised myself to walk like her towards the horizon and maybe learn not to look back.

Colder now, a cruel cold because I had known warmth, which I must now forget. Perpetual cold is kinder and so is unbroken silence. Keep to one present story then. For what does the memory of its old shape do for this new sand dune?

It was no dune. It was a large hill now that would take me a day to climb like Beenabe's hill before she was able to look to the other side.

From the peak, I saw more dunes, but smaller and endlessly changing shape. The wind was still restless. How I missed the one straight line of the horizon. I began my descent, wishing for certainty again.

The sun had almost set when I reached the dunes. Their shadows loomed over me. I began to walk faster, but the dunes seemed to multiply, and so did the shadows, walking just as fast. I was sure I could hear them following. I began to run.

Very soon everything became one shadow. Night had fallen and I was still running. I only slowed down when I heard a familiar sound. The tapping of spoons? Then I saw the first lights from a distance, moving forward and back, as if they were making up their minds then changing them with the constancy of the restless wind. They seemed to be leaving and returning to shadows darker than the night. I edged closer, but was stopped by a long, long line of twisted metal. I reached out, and cut myself. Barbed wire. It was a strangely wondrous hurt, a cut into memory, as I clambered up the sharp border towards a welcomed sight. Still shadows, like dunes of equal shapes and sizes, were tied to each other. No, they're tents, my brow urged me to remember. My breast leapt, grew warm. An old word was waking up there. *Home, home.* Then it went to sleep again as I heard only alien tongue from the tents and the men walking away from them and back, light cupped in their hands. But the way they looked up assured me they were my kin. Did they not trust the stars to help them digest their dinner? Someone told me that. Who? When?

I crept towards a tent and peeked inside. An old woman was beating a bowl with a spoon while a younger one, perhaps her daughter, licked it clean. Eyes closed, bodies rocking to the rhythm. Suddenly I was afraid for them and the walking men. I was desperate to warn them, but how and of what?

Then I sensed a shadow again, sneaking behind me. It grabbed my arm and pulled me down, muffling my scream with a hand on my mouth. 'Shhh ... shhh ... ' it hushed me, loosening its grip when I was finally calm.

This creature, whose speech I could not understand, felt damp and rough against me. When the light came on around its neck, I saw that it was afflicted with sores. It looked surprised when I did not recoil from its embrace. A jug soon appeared from under its blanket. It was offered to me and gratefully I drank. The creature almost wept in greater surprise, even joy. I said my thanks. It pounded its chest, whispering, 'Karitase, Karitase,' Then it washed my hands and feet, and only then did I realise I was bleeding from cuts, from my crossing over.

In the morning, I understood more. I found myself huddled with the afflicted woman on the road that led to the tents. She sat there offering her jug of water to everyone who passed, but no one drank. No one dared look at Karitase with her sores. All shrank away, hugging their blankets tightly around themselves, but the afflicted woman did not mind. She was listening to the song in my brow, even if she could not understand it.

'Please have no fear and
Take this offered hand
Your thirst, your thirst
Is my only affliction'

Louder than our alien tongues, our hands flailed to be understood, to make friends: I will not harm you, I am with you in this.

This was our wish for conversation. When faced with a stranger, we scare fear away with talk. When we find words to exchange, our hearts will not pound too much. When the shadows grew longer again, Karitase led me to the tent that perhaps she hoped could ease our hearts. We hid some paces outside, waiting for everything to become one shadow. Like me, she found the dark more friendly. No one stared in revulsion or looked away. Here she could pretend that I did not wear a singing locust on my brow, for she was still wary of it. Earlier she had looked at it in awe, then had drawn back but only for a moment. Then she let its wings graze her fingers, but also briefly. We were just getting to know each other.

Closer to the tent now, we waited until a low light came on inside. It smelled of the oil that now I knew so well. We watched as shadows began creeping in and out of the tent and different tongues were whispered, including my own. When all the shadows had left, Karitase began calling out in a pleading tone. From inside, a woman's voice answered and Karitase pushed me in.

I kept my head bowed, I kept myself small. I could not see who or what else were inside, not yet.

The woman spoke to me, not in my tongue, but I sensed a querying tone.

I shook my head.

She asked again, slipping to another strange tongue, then another, until finally she found the right one.

'I said, are you here for a story or a song?'

'Story — song?' I repeated, perplexed.

'Yes. I do story and song. But first, how much will you pay?'

Outside the tent Karitase began pleading again, causing the woman to ask me after a hostile pause, 'So you sing too?'

I was even more confused, especially with what sounded like protests from Karitase, until another light came on and she was hushed.

I could see better now. I made out a huge woman reclining among full pouches and jugs. I had never seen a woman with this sprawl of abundance. More lights came on, first on her hair, then around her ankles and wrists, even dangling from the lobes of her ears. She was wearing vials of light. She glowed. She looked me up and down and laughed. 'So, are you the competition?'

This was Shining Lumi and her multitude of lights. She never left her tent to queue for rations, but was always well fed. Here women from far and near queued with their share of rations as payment. Shining Lumi owned a skull that must be fed with seeds and oils and water, so it could sing the stories of the loved ones who disappeared in the wars or in their walk to the border, or in the ration line. Those who were *maybe dead.*

The skull sat on her breast. I knew its look so well.

'You do know that singing is a crime.'

The accusation glowed like her, I thought. For the first time I found my voice. 'No, I do not sing. Not really.'

'She who sings alone
Does not sing at all
A song is of someone
A song is for someone'

♪

The song brought Shining Lumi quickly to her feet. She panicked and kept hushing me, mumbling about traitor ears and mouths around, and about my stealing the duties of her skull. It had rolled off her breast towards where I was crouching. The skull stared at me, I stared back. I wanted to ask where the rest of its body was. I kept seeing the bones that I could not put back together again.

By the time Shining Lumi snatched the skull back to her bosom, she had already found out my secret. 'The plague,' she whispered. 'You're marked with the plague.'

Outside Karitase burst out in more protests and pleas, but the other woman argued, 'She means well? But you can't even understand her. She sounded good? Good songs cannot come from the plague.'

'Not the plague, but food. We ate it long ago.' My words came with a flood of saliva and the memory of crunching locusts, their sour-sweet taste with a hint of sand. Suddenly I felt the tiny wings beating in my brow, desperate to fly out. But the locust was as trapped as I was, and I could not even remember how or why our irrevocable kinship began.

'Those who feed on the plague are the plague.' Shining Lumi shuddered at my admission. 'You are what you eat.' Her ample flesh rippled with revulsion, then more accusations. 'So, Locust Girl, are you here to challenge me?'

When Shining Lumi asked this question, I stopped being Beena. I became the Locust Girl. After this renaming, no one would want to hear my old name again. Especially not my real name when I began remembering the older stories.

Unable to answer, I had to ask my own question. 'Why is singing a crime?'

'Why does *that* sing?' she countered.

'Why does anyone sing?' At that time, I believed that all had notes in their lungs and throat, and could naturally expel them like air. It did not occur to me that since I woke up in my hole, I had not heard anyone sing except my brow and those boxes, and the whispering youths in the ruins.

'And what do you sing anyway? I sing the truth, lest we

forget it. And who do you sing of? I sing of the lost ones, lest we forget them. And who do you sing for? I sing for those who seek them, lest we forget ourselves. Now can you sing any better?' Despite her dread, Shining Lumi was out to thrash what she saw as the rival of her precious trade.

But the truth was no songs were ever sung in this tent, only promises of songs perhaps tomorrow or tomorrow, when the skull was ready. Promises that were not even sung by Shining Lumi but only whispered in that mouth to ear ritual. 'Just between you and me, so keep it secret,' she'd order. Thus each supplicant believed that a special song about the lost beloved had been passed on to the one before her, and her turn would come when the skull was ready, if not today then tomorrow or tomorrow. Hope multiplied with the many tomorrows.

For Shining Lumi, trade was always good. The hopefuls kept coming. Her jugs were full, her pouches were fat.

'A seed for a song, my dear
And oil to grease the throat
Where I will find you safe
Breathing yet, breathing yet'

♪

Martireses and Nartireses were the first supplicants who heard my locust's song. They had been waiting for their turn outside the tent, while Shining Lumi tried to pin down my intentions. They could not believe that both of them had heard a song together, that it was sung aloud. It did not matter that it was sung in a strange tongue. Had the skull lost all caution? What if some traitor ear had heard it too? What if it got caught? What if they all got caught? What if they never found out the truth?

The twins were the most desperate supplicants of the skull. They came to hear the story about their father who had left for the border and never returned. Maybe this story can stop their ailing grandfather from his nightly to-ing and fro-ing under the stars, planning his own walk to the border to find his son. The twins were afraid he too would never return. They must keep another heartbreak at bay for the sake of their mother. So nightly they sneaked out of their tent to queue in all the ration lines, and to come here. The skull's waiting mouth was always hungry for seeds, water, and oil. They even traded for oil the only jewellery they'd shared since they left their mother's womb: the string of red beads that had tied their wrists together to seal their bond. They were special, their grandfather said, they were twins. Those red beads were saved from his mining days. The twins never took them off until one of them lost an arm at the rations. They never married. They barely ate, because the rations were for their elders and for the skull that promised to sing the true story.

They were not the only ones who walked into the tent that night. There was a girl in search of her mother who had disappeared while looking for a wedding gift for her daughter. There was a woman raving against the crime of rumours. There was a silent girl, a child, hiding under a blanket and the others protested that she was too young to be here until she brandished her fat pouches. There was a shaven youth with bruised arms and face. She had walked in shivering. There was a boy and an old man.

All of them had heard the song. They wanted to hear it again to make sense of it and to caution the skull against singing aloud.

At first there were loud protests: 'No men, no boys!' But the boy hopped about on one leg, waving his staff to demand his *own* song, and the old man with cuts on his head kept wringing his handless arms while the twins tried to calm him down.

Outside there was Karitase who had offered her jug of water to each of the supplicants, but with no success. She brought me here, so Shining Lumi could teach her my tongue and we could have a conversation. So she would know the song that my brow sang after I drank her offering. So she could hear it clearly in her heart.

♪

Beside ample flesh, all looked like skeletons holding their own lights, demanding to be served. I recognised Gurimar and Haraharan who refused to look at each other, the old man who had traded his blue stone and the beautiful youth with the bruised cheek, but with more bruises now.

'So the skull's singing, finally — but why so loud? We'll get caught.'

'It can keep its promise now.'

'I want my song now.'

'And mine — '

'You can't be here, grandfather.'

I heard anxious hope countered by another woman raving against rumours and the crime of singing. In the furthest corner of the tent, I tried to disappear among the shadows, but Cho-choli was right. *It* would betray me.

'Daily he walks to the blue skies
Nightly she dreams of yellow grain
His feet are nimble, her love is still
Their wish as constant as their will'

Everyone turned towards me. I pressed my hands to my brow but it kept singing in a way that I had never heard before. It took on the voice of a child, a woman, a man, an old woman, shifting through various timbres. The supplicants were stunned. They were hearing the voices of their lost ones! All gathered around me, even the children who were not calling me names now, even the woman raving her censure, even Shining Lumi who glowed in her ambivalence. Do I stop her, do I listen?

'Who wishes to dream first?
Who wishes to walk first?
Who wishes to drown
In song and never wake?'

'I want *my own* song, *my own* story!' This was the demand that plagued me, as did the hands that were all over me, except Shining Lumi and the children who knew about the mark of the plague. Even the old man sought me out with his stumps.

'Your own story is yours — tell it
Your own song is yours — sing it
Sing how lovely, how deadly
Is your dream of the border'

So many hands touching me. So much need, so much affection.

♪

Gurimar and Hara-haran: 4 pouches of seeds, 3 pouches of oil, no water
Inige: None (only silence)
Martireses and Nartireses: 2 pouches of seeds, 2 pouches of oil, 1 jug of water
Grandfather Opi: None (only despair)

Padumana: None (only protests)
Rirean: Half a pouch of oil

Regrettably, Shining Lumi did the accounting in her head. These payments were no longer hers. They had been laid at my feet, on everyone's and even my own blanket, now duly returned to me. I imagined Hara-haran had a change of heart and so did her brother, because of their unfinished business with me. Theirs was the loudest demand to hear their mother's voice again, to know where she is. The twins were not to be outdone, hurling queries at me, while their grandfather wept. Padumana's protests were as loud, so the soft-spoken Rirean could not be heard at all. Inige, 'the green tree', had buried her face in her hands.

With their blankets off and the gathered lights, I saw how different they were in appearance, in the shade of their skins. They came from different, faraway places. How far did they walk to get here? Hands still hiding my brow, I stared in wonder. So different, but they shared one earnest glow.

'You can all be tried for this. Singing is a crime!' Padumana's voice rose to a hysterical pitch. 'You don't know what it's like to be tried.'

'It's not us who are singing, so we're not breaking the law,' Rirean whispered. 'We just need to hear whether they're still alive and there's nothing wrong with that. Mother went walking to find a gift for my sister's wedding … maybe she walked too far.'

'That's it — we're walking too far in wanting to know,' Padumana argued. 'Trust me, it's better left alone — '

'How can we leave it alone — how can you leave it alone, huh? But of course, you don't have to drag yourself through the desert in search of your mother!' Hara-haran's rage was almost choking her.

'Don't you dare accuse me of leaving it alone!' Padumana grabbed the girl and began shaking her, but Gurimar's staff quickly pushed her away. Then he began beating her, egged on by most of the supplicants.

'Yes, beat me as they did,' and Padumana ripped off her wrap. 'Go on, exhaust yourself as my village did, as my family did. As if it matters now.'

Everyone froze. Padumana's back bore deep scars. She had been flayed to the bone. Her people did not punish by half-measures those who believed in rumours.

'Oh for the rumours of water, seeds, trees, colours, oh for the rumours about the other side, about lovers and kin, oh that they could be sung to ease our hearts,' Padumana wept.

'It's the murmur in the heart,' Inige whispered. 'The crime of rumour is the crime of hope.'

♪

We were all hushed. We turned to the whisperer. Her bruises made us wince.

'I have been through the border and back,' Inige began. 'I don't spread rumours, nor do I sing. But I can't deny the stories, just as I can't deny these bruises. Once I thought that by walking through the border, I could change it, just as the wind changes the desert.'

That night we saw the border through Inige's story. It made us hope, it made us want to weep.

'Its wall stretches forever like the horizon. It's a natural wall: a row of towering trees shielding the Five Kingdoms that hate real walls. The trees are pruned daily and their leaves polished so they can shine under the blue skies, oh how blue! The fathers are assigned to this task and they are always busy with no time for talk. They forgot about talk after they were arrested at the border. They had walked to the border to look for their children. Or maybe to wish for children in these barren times. But now the fathers have forgotten about children. They have been trained to love trees, oh how green! When the wind blows, the leaves sing and the fathers care for them as they would for children. Now no other story exists beyond this silent task. Sometimes their hearts murmur otherwise, and they find their tongue. They whisper rumours of the old stories, but they're quickly made to disappear, buried under the roots of the trees. So the trees are kept healthy and they live forever. So the border is evergreen. The border does not change.'

♪

Shining Lumi spoke in tongues, so everyone could understand Inige's story. Shining Lumi wanted her share of the payments. She knew how to adjust her trade, but somehow it did not give her the usual pleasure now.

The twins could not contain their despair after they heard the tale. 'That's a rotten rumour! Our father will never forget us.'

Inige sighed. 'I saw my own father and he did not recognise me.'

'Because you're a 'green tree' — all the fathers must have taken care of you,' Gurimar sneered. 'So how much were you paid to open your legs?'

'I'm a father and I will never forget my son,' Grandfather Opi cried. 'Did you see him, oh did you see a man with clear eyes and a limp?'

'And what about the mothers?' Hara-haran asked, fearful now.

Inige closed her eyes as if she could not bear to see her next story. 'Among more trees called woods, the mothers are suckling newborn animals whose own mothers were killed by hunters for their silken fur. The mothers suckle the orphans with their blood, because there's no milk in their breasts. Soon these orphans are also killed for their fur. The mothers bury little bloody mounds. Some feed on them secretly. The hunters ask the mothers to wash afterwards. The woods have endless water called rivers flowing into each other. The hunters take the mothers deeper into the woods. Their breasts are bared to bait more orphans. The mothers do the task of suckling and burial again. Their breasts dry up like their eyes.'

♪

Hara-haran acted first. She lunged for Inige's neck, screaming, 'Liar!' Gurimar raised his staff. The twins joined in the beating. Grandfather Opi and Rirean pleaded with the storyteller to recant. Padumana chanted, 'Leave it alone, leave it alone!'

Shining Lumi looked on, but she could not leave it alone in her head. She had never left her tent where she saw only humble supplicants huddled together for comfort. She had never seen despair this ugly, just unbearably painful for the eyes. Sometimes it made her whisper the skull's promises in colour: mothers and fathers and sons and daughters and all loved ones are well under blue skies, among green trees and red flowers and orange birds that sing of homecomings soon, soon.

'How could you spread rotten rumours? Who are you trying to fool? Were you paid by the Five Kingdoms? What woods, what rivers, what towering trees? How can our fathers forget us? How can our mothers have blood in their hands? How can you mock us?'

The supplicants had thrust the skull towards Inige's face. The gaping mouth seemed to be asking the questions. I kept screaming for them to stop, but I could barely hear myself. The tapping spoons had begun again. Outside the men were to-ing and fro-ing under the stars.

'How beautiful is hope'

'You don't understand,' Inige cried.

'How deadly a beauty'

The skull stared as if it understood.

'We are in the border'

Karitase crept in to offer her water.

'Before we even get there?'

My brow sang on. For once, it sounded unsure.

They turned to me again and saw. I could no longer hide it. The sight of the creature on my brow stopped the beating. Everyone shrank away. I crept towards Inige and tried to raise her. I feared she was dead. Now in the tent, Karitase brought her jug to the victim's mouth. My brow began singing again in the voices of the lost ones. Instinctively everyone took a step towards us then shrank away again. Have they killed her? Will they be punished now with *that* plague? Quickly they retrieved their offered payments, their eyes on the locust singing in my brow.

Shining Lumi could not leave it alone any longer. She took a jug of her oil and began soothing Inige's fresh bruises. I remembered the man with the blue stone around his neck.

All the supplicants gathered around our ritual of making better. Shining Lumi ministered with her oil, Karitase, with her water. Shining Lumi glowed with her lights, Karitase kept to the shadows. Shining Lumi had known trust, Karitase, only revulsion. They did not want to like each other, but — they refused to think about it. They refused to think at all as they cared for Inige who did not seem to mind the sores on the hands that washed the blood from her brow. Everyone else was afflicted with ambivalence. The fear of the plague and the hope for the lost ones argued against each other. But they were certain of one thing. They wanted the 'green tree' alive.

Still barely conscious, Inige traced my brow with a finger, querying the form of the plague, then the sores on Karitase's hand. I heard a shudder from the circle of onlookers who kept their distance. Then someone cleared her throat, followed by another, then another. I thought of the remorseful sounds from Just-me-uhm. Even Shining Lumi cleared her throat, awkwardly apologising for the act. 'It's the ill wind and the sand it carries, you know. Hurts the throat.'

Their breathing was as desperate as the rhythm of spoons rippling the other tents, just as the wind rippled the dunes further away. I heard them, I heard hope to-ing and fro-ing under the stars. The wind picked up these rumours and carried them through a huddle of tents, through the sand dunes and to the ruins, to the ears of Just-me-uhm and his men. The wind is a faithful messenger for all. Something in my bones told me I had to warn this village about it or about something that rode on its tail. Something more than sand.

'The wind knows no border
The wind takes no sides
The wind betrays none
The wind betrays all'

♪

An ill wind could only bring ill rumours. Back in the ruins, Just-me-uhm heard and dreaded them. They led to one bad turn after another. He knew that from the past. Since the rations began, he had cleared his throat with painful constancy at each meal. His men soon picked up his habit. Quxik, his lackey, cleared his throat louder than the others.

I heard them then, did I not? Their conspiracy of throats was also carried back by the wind to our tent?

Short, squat and without a neck, Quxik was built like a fighter. He thought like a fighter. He was quick with his head and quicker with his hands. Did he not slap that silly whisperer before she had convinced the others to escape? But his sillier chief had to soothe her cheek — hypocrite! Quxik scorned Just-me-uhm's waverings, his contrite clearing of the throat, which he himself could not get rid of now.

Quxik was also a bastard of the Five Kingdoms, but unlike Just-me-uhm, he had not severed ties with his own father, the Minister of Arms. Quxik was the minister's most valued spy. He told all to his father. He had already told him about the ill rumours many dunes away, even if Just-me-uhm had begged him to sit these out this time. Because the ill wind will pass — what stupidity! The truth was his chief was terrified of the 'bad turns of fate.'

Quxik hated his chief's father most. The Minister of Mouths

had airs — hah, he was nothing but a voice, a pretentious mouth! Quxik was convinced that the singing minister scorned his father, the Minister of Arms, because he did not have the gift of tongue. No glib poise, he didn't need it. His father worked silently but with precision. 'What would the Five Kingdoms be without a fine man to protect us all?' Did the Honourable Head not say this of his father at one public dinner? But the Minister of Mouths had to sing the Missions over that praise, and of course all turned to him again even if it was no longer fashionable to sing the Missions at the table. No one could resist *that* voice.

Quxik cleared his head as much as his throat. He will not let petty stories get in the way. He has a duty to the Five Kingdoms. He had sent a message to his father about the ill wind from a village of strays: They're walking again and there's even some singing. The border is under threat. The Five Kingdoms are under threat. We are under threat, so unleash the peace fire. Let the ill wind fan it beyond the dunes.

He made sure the Minister of Mouths heard the message too. Let him lose his glib poise at the thought that the lowly folk, those strays, have infiltrated his singing domain. Let his voice croak as it always does in anger. Let him go off-key.

In the tent, Grandfather Opi cleared his throat with no hint of apology. 'My throat's not hurting, my throat's getting ready — just getting ready to sing, and so are all of you. We're just clearing it down there, you know. Because there's too much dust or too much sand down there, like an old grave.'

Grave. I remembered how it sounded like a nothing word the first time I heard it from Beenabe. 'This is no longer your home Beena, this is a *grave*.'

'Dig up that grave, stop the Five Kingdoms from burying our lives, from burying us alive. I'm a very old man, I won't have long to live, my life should not be cut shorter by burying all that went before it — ' and the old man started wheezing so hard that he doubled over on the ground. He kept pounding his chest with his stumps to wake up the wind in there.

His granddaughters came to the rescue, chiding him. 'Grandfather, you shouldn't have come, you should go home and rest.'

'Home and rest — are these all that an old man is good for?' In between wheezes, he waved his stumps while gulping for air. 'I won't be buried alive and the oldest story won't be buried with me.'

The twins retrieved their water payment and made him drink it. They rubbed his chest with oils until the wheezing stopped. All of us waited for it to stop. We waited to hear the oldest story. Even Inige sat up to hear it better. Grandfather Opi had heard it from his father who heard it from his father, who heard it from his father. In their own time, they did not have to clear their throats to tell this story.

'Once upon a time, there were countries with their own fields of grain and seeds to plant for each season, and endless waters and animals that drank in them, and oils gushing from wells, and beautiful colours not only in dreams. And children, there were plenty of children then. But each of the countries secretly wished to control all grains and seeds, all waters and animals, all oils, all colours, even all dreams, so they fought each other with great fires. So there was much devastation and despair. So the bigger countries embraced each other to become the biggest and strongest country with the greatest fire.

Soon the biggest country directed the greatest fire towards the smaller countries to end all petty fires. The Minister of Arms took care of the sky and the air. He made new winds as he waved his powerful limbs. It all became very confusing especially for the earth. It began to dry up and all the countries dried up, but not the biggest one, because the Minister of Mouths began singing to clear the confusion. His songs directed the grains and the seeds and the waters and the oils and the animals and the colours and the dreams towards the biggest country, to preserve them for the future. Then the Minister of Legs began to direct the lost peoples from the lost countries to their new homes. The lucky ones found their way to the biggest country where they were re-settled as dutiful carers of the earth. Some were given villages of huts or tents, but the others have been walking the dry earth for the rest of their lives to find a home. To avoid any more confusion, the Honourable Head drew a clear line between the biggest country and the rest of the earth. He promised that this line would save the human race. So now we have the border keeping us from the last remaining country, the last green home on earth: the Five Kingdoms. The Kingdom of Waters, the Kingdom of Seeds, the Kingdom of Oils, the Kingdom of Colours, the Kingdom of Fires.'

Grandfather Opi's story rode on his wheezing lungs, so the telling sounded like a strange singing. I remembered Cho-choli's stories riding on her sighs and tears.

♪

When Inige began breathing evenly again, Grandfather Opi's lungs filled with fresh air from a green field long ago. He remembered older rhythms: the rise and fall of notes akin to the rise and fall of breath. He began to really sing. He sang about how it was before the big dry. He sang the colours vividly. He sang the taste of fresh water from the springs, and golden grains, and meat from the animals that grazed among the green. He sang of his father and mother, and how it was to have two hands as a boy. He sang of his wedding with his childhood sweetheart, the birth of their son and that of his twin granddaughters, and the red beads with which he joyfully bound their wrists after they left their mother's womb. He sang how he found the beads and many more beautiful stones. He sang the colours underground, how they glowed even in the darkness of the mines. He sang how he lost his hands, but began to wheeze again, to lose air, so his granddaughters picked up his tune and remembered how their father used to kiss them goodnight, how the kiss was a whisper of 'green', 'blue', 'red' on their brows so they could dream in colour, how he added new colours before he left for the border, but at this note, the twins' voices broke, so Padumana repaired their song with her own memory about the birth of her sons at the time when she thought she had dried up like the earth, how her sons grew up on daily hunger and thirst and how they joined the village in beating her because of her rumours of hope, and here Padumana's song faltered, she could not go on, not with Hara-haran's cry against the blood in the hands of mothers who buried dead animals in the woods, but her brother Gurimar muffled her cry with the story of only one mother putting on a necklace of seeds and pushing down her wrap to reveal half of her dry bosom, and primping up what remained of her hair, while telling her son to go home, promising she would follow soon and bring plenty of seeds and water and oil, and maybe some meat which he had never seen before, and she kept walking and smiling towards a group of men on their way to the border, her shoulders thrown back and her hips with a peculiar sway, how Gurimar loved her then as much as he hated her, but Rirean quickly censured his memory, remembering her own mother who left to find a wedding present for her sister after she had blessed her womb already heavy with child, saying the ill wind was maybe turning now and the dry spell was breaking, but the wedding was tomorrow and still her mother hasn't returned, so Rirean slept with her sister's groom to pay for half a pouch of oil to pay for the skull to sing about her mother and where she is now, while secretly wishing she owned her sister's womb, then finally Inige's secret ended the communal song, and she sang of dreams turning into nightmares, of stories turning inside out and words changing meanings to break the heart.

It was the longest song after a very long time of silence.

By now the tapping spoons had long faded in the other tents. The stars had begun hiding. The walking men were returning to their tents. But their ears picked up something never heard before from our tent in the outskirts of the village — was it a new wind? It made them stop. It made them remember how to clear their throats. It made them remember how to sing.

Back in the ruins, Just-me-uhm worried about how to keep the ill wind from the border. He needed to fortify it, not so much in his head but in his heart that was fluttering uncertainly, as if the ill wind was already lurking there. So he thought long thoughts —

Faraway, in the last green place on earth, lives a harmony of all colours. They love and respect the purity of natural things, which they guard with their lives (so honourable). They believe these are dangerous times and they could lose the very scarce gifts of the earth: water, food, oil and even clean air. Thus they built a border between the *carers* and the *wasters* (so wise). To keep life simple, countries were dismantled and the basic gifts were given to everyone according to everyone's capacity to care for them. The world is a more equal village now (I'm grateful). Rewards are given where rewards are due. Because of their wisdom and caring values, the carers can live freely with the gifts and trade in them. The wasters have to be 'managed': cared for and rationed. They must be protected from themselves, as history dictates. They are profligate and dangerous, as history proves (I studied history as a child). The wasters are always plotting to waste more, or, worse, to steal what the carers worked so hard to preserve. The Five Kingdoms even preserved the history of our poor earth in their books, but refuse to invoke it now. All must move on and contend with the present. The present is about protecting the border.

Just-me-uhm's thoughts were gathered from the Five Kingdoms. They sounded strange in his head, as if spoken in another tongue, but he thought them anyway. His throat hurt with each thought, so he had to clear it, just as he had to clear his head with little asides.

All colours are respected in the Five Kingdoms (that's equality). They trade with each other, make friends, and even sing together in their own tongues at public rituals, but they keep their beds pure (that's wisdom). There is harmony in purity and purity in harmony. White is as white as driven snow; black is as ebony fine as the night. Brown is the vigour of mountains; yellow is the royal hue of the sun. And red is the pride of blood and bloodline. This is how the Kingdoms see and speak of themselves: in natural terms (natural is good). But they try not to speak too much of colour. They worry about using the wrong inflections on this or that colour. They worry about offending the ear. Carers are careful people; they check themselves and each other all the time (so they should). For reasons of safety and preservation, they check more rigorously those who live at the other side of the border (so we should).

These long thoughts made Just-me-uhm nervous and unsure. They made him ask: *What side of the border am I?* He worked in ruins and wretched deserts outside the Kingdoms. His mother was of this wasteland. But when he went through the border for his earned rest from rationing, when he lazed under the bluest skies of the Five Kingdoms and ate of their fruit, the question was quickly forgotten. When he thought of how his father made him chief of rationing, he felt ashamed of the question. When he remembered how the Minister of Mouths sang him lullabies as a child, he recovered his trust: indeed he belonged to the *right* side of the border.

♪

In the tent, my brow continued the song of the supplicants. It sang in all tongues harmonising together. Different cadences conspired. Different inflections counterpointed perfectly.

'The wind in the lungs
Is the only wind to trust
It is what turns the sand
It is what turns the tide'

The walking men never returned to their tents. The women and their handful of children never went to sleep. They gathered in our tent. When day finally broke, we trusted the wind in our lungs. For three days, we sang our stories.

Back in the ration camp, the rumour of singing was too

much to bear for Just-me-uhm. It was his turn to to scour the earth. He had to stop another bad turn of fate, having seen too many in his time. For three days, he crossed the desert to find us.

Just-me-uhm's departure pleased Quxik immensely. It was his turn to be chief. It was his father's turn to be proud. In three days, all will come to pass.

On the third day, we sang at the wedding of Rirean's sister. We marvelled at the bride's ripe belly. We thought she was beautiful.

♪

Before the vows, the wind began brewing up a storm. Decked in garlands of seeds and brows glowing with oil, the bride and groom held on to each other lest they were blown away. We all held on to each other. We shut our mouths tightly to keep the sand out. We ended our songs. But our spirits were up. Grandfather Opi kept whispering, 'Better a sandstorm than the fires of war, you know … we can forgive the wind, the sand …'

The wind howled. The pregnant Trapsta billowed even bigger in the arms of her groom Silam. This child will be the first after ten years of dryness in the clan. It will bear the name of the bride's lost mother: Unre.

♪

On the dunes' endlessly changing shape, Just-me-uhm saw a crowd of bodies swaying with the wind. His eyes picked up the bride and groom. He picked up her swollen belly and his throat hurt. Then the first ball of fire hit the wedding party. He would never be able to clear his throat again after that. He found himself running towards the screaming crowd running from the conflagration. 'I lost sight of the bride, I lost sight of the bride,' was all he could hear in his head, until a song rose from the fires.

'Beloved, forgive me
Love is clumsy because
It has so many hands
It has so many hands'

LOVE

And then

Arms snatched me out of the fire, and I remembered Beenabe running towards a conflagration, then the howling, louder than the wind's, then the smell of charred bodies, until finally in the furthest corner of my skull, I found the story hidden for thirteen years. The night the stars went out over five hundred tents. The night my father walked towards the horizon and never returned.

'I'm Amedea, daughter of Abarama and I want my father, I want my father.' My head was bursting with my want, even as a voice soothed me, even as arms tightened around me, shielding me from the heat and the howling, oh that most horrific song.

'I'm 425a, daughter of 425, it's on his neck, beneath the ear, the blue number — '

'Hush, hush,' the strong arms crooned. Then the pounding, a heart about to leap out of the chest, but it wasn't mine. Are you my father? Did you come home from your walk under the stars to save me? Have you digested your dinner? Are the stars burning? Will they burn out and leave me in the dark? 'You won't leave me, say you won't leave me — '

'No, child, I'm taking you to a safe place.'

'Is it green with trees?'

'Yes, yes.'

'With blue skies above?'

'It's all colours.'

'Oh father, how beautiful. Not like me.'

'Go away, leave us alone,' my father said, but they continued to stalk us. The shafts of darkness hovered like long arms ready to snatch me away and the beams of light flashed about as if to expose this abduction. Or maybe they needed to witness it, because I was unable to do so now. My eyes had shut, but his voice left me a window into the world of the living.

'She's mine, you can't have her,' he said, addressing the shadow and light.

I am his, I am my father's child.

'It was *not* me, I was only doing my job, I took care of all of you.'

You scoured the desert for locusts, you fed me.

'I can't take care of all of you now.'

It's all right, father.

'Don't look at me like that. Of course, I can walk away from this, I'm walking away from this.'

The wind had returned to its lair, but the light and shadow continued to loom over us silently. They entered my lids and my mouth that had so much to say. It wanted to answer his query even if it didn't know how.

'Is it possible, my change of heart?'

Everything is possible, father. Everything.

I will never know how long we walked with me in his arms. But I knew I was fed with seeds and water and soothed with oils, and that the trail of light and shadow never left us. We walked to his mutterings in different voices and tongues.

Even women's voices? There were moments when I thought it was the creature in my brow up to its old trick but not in song this time.

'Give me more seeds — '

'I can't, the child needs them.'

'Have some of my water — '

'I can't — '

'Because you're afraid you'll catch her affliction.'

'I'm not afraid.'

'Or that you'll catch the plague. But the plague is already in your arms, or didn't you know?'

He can't see the mark on my brow? Was it burned out of me?

'Shhh … let her sleep.'

'As if the plague sleeps.'

'She has a name, or didn't you hear?'

'Of course. She is the Locust Girl.'

'I'm sure we all have names — I am Verompe.'

Not Abarama? Where is my father? But how could I ask? My mouth had also shut by then.

'I'm Karitase, and this is Shining Lumi — let the child have some of my water, please.'

They're alive, my friends are alive!

Of course, Shining Lumi never left her tent for anything, not even a wedding, and Karitase was banned from it lest the bride and groom were cursed by her affliction. So they were saved. But Trapsta, Silam, Gurimar, Hara-haran, Inige, Padumana, Rirean or the twins and their grandfather … somewhere in a far corner of my skull, I was back at the wedding, in the belly of the great fire.

'No, leave her face alone, Verompe, sir. Let the child cry.'

Karitase, dear Karitase, I know now. Not one of them was

saved, not one of them.

'Looks worse than before — you think she'll live?'

Ah, Shining Lumi with her uncertain concern.

'Of course, she'll live,' and Verompe held me tighter. He had strong arms and gentle hands. They were generous with the oils. His chest smelled both gritty and aromatic. Maybe he even oiled his heart.

Squeaky clean and flexible. Is this how a heart should be? Not the anguished pounding earlier or this creaking against my cheek. Ah, the heart's rusty, that's why he oils his chest, that's why I'm swooning even in my sleep. I love this sweet embrace and I won't let his mutterings bother me.

'This is for all the children who were turned away, for all the children ...'

I did not doubt it. Verompe was speaking to me, but Shining Lumi took it upon herself to respond. 'What children? There are hardly any these days?'

'Because they were turned away, but I can't tell you more, my throat hurts.'

'Here, sir, drink some of my water.'

But I knew hardly anyone drank from Karitase's jug.

'Where are you from anyway? I've never seen you before.'

'Best not to ask, Shining Lumi,' he answered.

'Where are you taking us, sir?'

'I'm only taking her, Karitase,' and Verompe quickly shifted away. I imagined Karitase had crawled to us in a suppliant gesture. I felt the moistness of her sores against my skin. It cooled my burnt flesh.

'If you take her, you take us too. We're her kin.' Shining Lumi never missed a beat with her inventions.

'Are you?'

'We're her aunties — '

'No, we're her friends,' Karitase protested.

I wanted to say, of course, I drank from your jug and my locust sang to you, and you didn't run away, and strange, I understand you now, Karitase, I understand all of you. The fire has tuned my ear to all tongues.

'She's her friend but I'm her auntie, the youngest sister of her mother who moved to another village when my niece was born. We only caught up a few days ago when she visited me in my tent, so I can't just let her go, can I? You have to take me with you,' Shining Lumi insisted.

My mother was a tall and proud tree, her name was Alkesta and she smelled of wind and sand — and she has a sister who wears lights on her ample body? That's a nice lie or a kind rumour that I still belong to someone in the world of the living.

'As an auntie, I can't let a stranger take my niece without me, of course.'

Who said I was asleep? I simply could not open my eyes. But I heard them clearly. I heard the secret flexing of their hearts.

Why don't you sing the sound of feet? Why don't you multiply them like you did with the dripping water? But no one answered up there. I was convinced the creature in my brow had died, burned out of me in that fire. Suddenly I felt I was only half of my old self with so little to add to the steps on the sand. So few, so few. I wanted to leave his arms and add my own. I wanted a multitude of walking feet. I wanted more than five hundred skulls and bones to put themselves together again and walk out of the fire and the desert. I wanted all the ration lines to take the trail. Even the dragging feet will leave this wretchedness. Even the legless will reach the green border. I wanted to say all these to the women behind us, especially to Shining Lumi who kept complaining that her feet hurt and how long will this walking go for anyway.

'Here, Lumi, take my hand.'

'Keep away, Karitase.'

'Your legs are not strong, you've stayed too long in that tent.'

'It was my duty as it was my mother's and her own mother's. We stayed put while others walked, so they'd have a place to come home to for hope. I come from the promise line and I'm proud of it.'

'Yes, the promise of homecoming of their maybe dead,' Karitase sighed.

'It's what they lived for — '

'And died for.'

And you traded on their hope, I wanted to add, but there was no more room for unkindness then. The desert was unkind enough. I tried to imagine Shining Lumi taking Karitase's hand, and the light and shadow finally bonded like the twins with their red beads. And indeed under my lids, I dreamt I saw Martireses and Nartireses following in even strides with Grandfather Opi at their heels. Then Padumana and Inige with their scars, and then Rirean leading Gurimar with Hara-haran on his back, and behind them the wedding party leading the longest ration line leading five hundred families, the fathers with their lights, the mothers with their spoons tapping on bowls as steadfast as their pulse, and following them, all the strays since the beginning of time, from wherever their home that was lost, all of us walking in despair and hope towards the border.

I was sure we were walking together under the stars. Then my saviour and I were lifted up — who knows when those winking lights landed with a giant locust whirring 'blessed, blessed'? But a voice argued in my head: 'Not a locust but a plane, Beena.' I wanted to argue back as we flew. Why are we leaving everyone behind? Are we the only blessed ones? But no sound came from my mouth. Soon the brown of the sky faded. When I woke up, I thought maybe the sky was never brown at all.

Blue can blind but green can make you see again. Blue fire assaulted my eyes, I had to shut them tight. Had I not seen that brilliant blue before? But not this close. I felt the strong arms lay me down, I heard receding steps. When I opened my eyes again, I felt as if they were just being born. They opened wider and wider to this thing above me that seemed to open even my chest, so my heart could share the feast. I started crying with my first vision of a green tree.

A tree. Thus my saviour explained while thoughtfully rubbing the blue stone around his neck, then it all came back to me. I saw everything again as clearly as the green canopy. The blue stone for seeds. The whipping of the whisperers. The soothing of Inige's cheek and Grandfather Opi's battered head. The stone winking blue fire on the night of the rations and the voice that turned children away. But I had to pretend ignorance. Even if now I was all of twenty-two, to his eyes I was a child and I was at his mercy.

'Breathtaking, isn't it? I used to cry too each time I saw a tree after months in the desert.' The last words were barely audible, as if he did not want me to hear them. This close, how beautiful he looked and he glowed — his hair, his skin, especially his eyes as blue as the stone around his neck. 'Up there are the leaves and branches, the leaves are green, the branches brown, and this is the trunk, it's brown too — breathtakingly beautiful.'

Like my mother Alkesta. Tall and proud as a tree. But I had no time to dwell on the thought. I checked for his whip. He did not have it around his waist. I wanted to plead, don't hurt me, but could not find my voice. Suddenly from a distance, an unfamiliar sound. He followed my fearful eyes with his own as I took in rows of trees overwhelming in their greenness, but no movement there. He could see I was hearing something. Then it was gone. I turned to him again. He looked relieved as he whispered, 'I brought you fruit.'

I flinched. The ball shone on his hand. I waited for it to hit me. Surely he caught me spying in the ruins or did I just imagine it? Will he remember?

'It's for eating, it's an apple — you've never seen one?' He sighed at my lack of response. When he spoke again, his voice was thick with apology. 'Of course, not.' He touched his throat and swallowed painfully.

'Here,' he said, pushing the shining ball close to my mouth which I clamped tight. I tried to rise, but he pushed me down. He must have seen the panic in my eyes. 'I won't hurt you, you're safe. Just-me will take care of you, I promise,' then he bit into the ball. 'It's food, a red apple, you'll like it.'

Red. What comes out of you if you prick yourself.

Tenderly he fed me with the bit from his mouth. An apple. I remembered another saviour handing me a seed. 'Chew it, it will make you feel better,' because she felt better by making me feel better, like this man who smiled as I chewed and swallowed through my tears.

Did you hear that? I forced myself to sit up despite his protests. I could see he heard nothing, but there it was again. A warning from long ago, like whisperings from the ruins or a whirring from the grave. Instinctively I touched my brow. Was *it* still alive? But my brow felt smooth under my fingers now.

Then, another sound and something hit me, and I saw the red stain on my chest, as bright as the apple that had rolled out of my hand. Quickly he gathered me and broke into a run. Behind us I saw something covered in the same stain and in agony on the ground also green, and then the trees were a blur as he ran, whispering, 'It's not you, it's not you, it's an amber guri, shot with an arrow.'

Amber. Guri. Arrow. Apple. Too much to take in and too little time.

How we got up the thickest tree, I couldn't tell. From up there, we watched as the guri was skinned by a woman in bright clothes. Then the amber fur was thrown into a pouch and the carcass was buried, but only after she had eaten most of it. Inige's story. The mothers with blood on their hands.

He turned my face away from the sight below towards the vision of the last green haven on earth. Shock and repulsion did not have a chance to settle in. My eyes feasted. There were green trees everywhere and other colours, which, I learned later, were fields of grain and fruit and flowers — and water! Like the endless water of Cho-choli, but this one sparkled and flowed peacefully, promising sweetness under the blue sky. Then there were the towers that a long time ago my father had promised I would see when I was ready. When I had grown up big and strong and good.

Amidst this plenty was a large circle of trees where people in bright clothes were beginning to gather, forming shapes around a single tree, the biggest and tallest of them all. The shapes were the colour of the clothes sorted into groups, as the man who held me explained: a red circle, a blue square, a green triangle repeated here and there. I remembered the shapes that Beenabe and I drew with our feet as we walked around a thin boulder of sand, but our shapes were brown and drab.

I felt my head swim. Here they were, rumours of colour confirmed and jostling my heart towards many directions. My chest ached, my breath could not keep up with my wonder. Any moment my heart would protest and stop. How could anyone live with too much beauty and plenty, and not feel like dying?

Then I heard again the whisperings. Only, I was wrong about the source of the sound. This was the crowd's multitude of tongues, which grew louder and which now I understood so well, perhaps because I knew the thought so well:

'Lest we forget —
There is only one story
There is only one song
That we take home'

Then the words rose as a song, but in just one voice and in that same tune from the blue box in the ruins. But the *one story* was different.

'Peace. Purity. Piety. Preservation.' The chant of the multitude made my brow itch, made my cheeks tingle. Their words rose with their arms towards the tallest, oldest tree on earth.

His arms tightened around me. Just-me-uhm was weeping, Verompe was weeping (How should I call him now?). He had not heard his father sing that song since he was six, or was it five, except from boxes.

Amid the chant, three children circled the tree. Later I would find out that they were not children but the ancient and shrunken ministers sprinkling some powder on the roots of the tree. To bless it and preserve its life. To make it grow big and strong and good. Then there was a minute's silence after which the Minister of Mouths sang the Missions, ending with much rejoicing.

'You are ours

You are part of Kingdom building'

My saviour wept even more. Later he told me that the following speech never failed to make everyone weep in this yearly festival. The Honourable Head always spoke with graciousness and no one could help the flow of tears.

'My fellow Kingdom builders,' the Head began, addressing everyone as equals. 'There is peace if the border is protected. There is purity if all keep to their own place under their own sky. And piety comes with the strict observance of caring values that preserve the human race and its home: the Five Kingdoms. And lest we forget, the gifts of the Kingdoms are preserved for the *carers* of the natural world. The *wasters* have no place in this new order, those breeders who consumed and dried up nature with their profligate ways long ago. Those who wasted even each other so cruelly and foolishly. But out of the goodness of our hearts, out of our love for justice and everyone's equal right to be free to enjoy the blessed earth, a right equal only to the caring effort contributed, we care even for the wasters.'

The burst of applause made all the trees, even ours, tremble. The man who held me was trying to keep his own hands from clapping. His face shone with pride while I felt dumb. I could not follow the words of the Honourable Head. They were moving towards too many roads all at once.

'So how do we uphold this ideal of preservation in our hearts? How do we keep the peace in our homes?'

The murmured response was too familiar.

'No one should look

No one should walk beyond the horizon'

Again the words rose in a song of the single resonant voice that could no longer be left unacknowledged.

'That's my father singing, that's my father!' my saviour cried, declaring his heritage. I heard pride and longing all at once.

'Long ago, he used to sing to me,' he added.

I tried to remember whether my own father ever sang. The trying made my head ache, then itch and whirr, then echo the song to perfection.

'You sing? You know the song too?' he asked in wonder.

I touched my brow but it was not coming from there. The song was inside my skull now. Verompe put a finger to his lips then motioned towards the ground. More women in bright clothes were burying bloody mounds at the roots of trees. The leaves quivered even more in the hands of men polishing each leaf. Soon we realised that even our tree had its own caretaker. For a moment he stared at us, then turned away, resuming his silent task.

I heard a soft crackle but could not make out what it was. I was not yet familiar with the sound of trees. I did not know that the caretaker had secretly crushed a leaf in his hand and the gesture was echoed further away among the tree worshippers. A squat man, who was built like a fighter, was quick with his ears and hands. He heard the crackle. It was a signal. Discreetly he picked up a fallen leaf from the great tree and crushed it too. A few paces away, his father, the Minister of Arms, picked up the message: strays had crossed the border.

Crushing a leaf. Much later, I understood this gesture of warning. The tree caretakers were trained lookouts. Once they were strays themselves. They had walked from the desert to the border. Inige said they were looking for their children. Some, yes, but the truth was most were lured by the rumours of water and seeds and colours. Others were driven by queries about why the rations were drying up. Did they just dream up the promises of those who had built pipes into their wells to preserve their water and oil in a faraway place? Was it only a nightmare — how the fires had dried up their villages, their fields of grain, the wombs of their women? Or was it a rumour whispered from mouth to ear and mouth to ear through the hungry years?

Those years were over. Now they had their fill of the Kingdoms' grains, though they were not allowed to touch any of the animals. Meat was only for those born in the Kingdoms, because these true carers can regulate their feeding according to the Minister of Mouths. This edict did not worry the guardians of the trees. At least their hunger was over. The more they fed, the more the queries and the rumours and the dreams were pushed from their hearts to make room for the love of trees. Here, they had been trained to labour faithfully. Each leaf shone. Each leaf became a mirror. It crackled signals with efficient certainty. Strays were caught with ease. The wall of trees, this green border, was always safe. The Five Kingdoms preserved its peace.

On this yearly festival of the adoration of the tree, the caretakers worked with more fervour. This was the chance to show off their skill and loyalty to the masters. To prove that they were part of Kingdom building. One day, they will belong. Maybe they will even be allowed to eat meat. They will grow roots. They will be home. Blessed are the peacekeepers for theirs are the Kingdoms.

Verompe. Just-me-uhm. The names kept changing places in my head as we walked, eating fruit that seemed to grow everywhere. He carried me away from that tree, saying we were no longer safe. We had been seen, we had to walk through the tall grasses. I was slowly gaining the use of my legs, but not my voice. I had so much to say and ask. As we stumbled into bits of fur and blood and fresh graves, I wondered if the mothers could ever wash the blood from their hands. I felt my chest. The stain was dry but seemed indelible.

When night fell, we found ourselves before the biggest water and a huge shining stone, half in the water, half in the sky.

'No, it's a full yellow moon rising from the water,' he said. 'It betrays everything. We should hide where the grass is thickest to pass the night. Trees are not safe here.'

He taught me how to cup my hands and drink in the Kingdom of Waters. We drank so much, I wondered whether we would also drink up the moon. Then he said he must clean my burns and wash off the stain on my chest. He must wash even the desert off me to avoid any detection.

Why are you doing this? Why did you save me? Why was I saved and not the others? Did the great fire spit me out? Could it not stomach my scarred body? And you — how could you bear touching an ugly stray? But of course I had no way to ask him yet. I had lost my speech. I let him take me into the water, washing me then himself. Lit by the moon, his naked body was even more beautiful. I stared. He caught my eye and plunged deeper. Then he went behind a tree where he dressed himself. For the first time, I noticed that the insides of his shirt were lined with pouches of oil and seeds, and even a long blue smock that he unfolded and made me wear. How fitting the colour. I wanted to tell him about my village of five hundred blue tents and the blue numbers beneath our ears that kept track of our walking, our living.

The bath made my whole body sting, but quickly it was soothed with oils. Was I healing so soon? His hands were tender though not as certain with their strokes. Was it because I had seen him naked? He was shaking slightly as he rubbed oil over my burns. Then he told me his name and I pretended to hear it for the first time. He told me about fishes and I wondered about pink prawns. He told me about the shy animals that came to drink only at night and I strained my ears to hear them. He told me about birds that were banished because their singing confused the songs of Kingdom building. He lay me down among the tall grasses and I wanted him to lie down with me. He stretched his body an arm's length away and I wanted to snuggle close. Then he told me how this biggest water made trees and grasses green and I wondered if it made the apple red. He praised how the Kingdoms cared for this water as they cared for their own lives, and I wanted to ask how they called it. Was it riverrrr with a delicate roar, or ocean with a ssshh that hushed them to sleep at night? Then we watched the moon climb, leaving the water and losing its yellow sheen.

Deep into the night, the leaves continued to shine like mirrors. They caught our sleeping bodies in their tiny frames.

'Where did you learn to sing? Why is it that you can't speak but you can sing?' He grabbed my shoulders, shook me. 'Are you playing tricks on me?'

I wondered whether it sang through my sleep. I was grateful that his need to know was not bound with hate or despair, unlike Hara-haran when she insisted to hear the truth about a lullaby.

He let go of me, turned away. 'But I — ' there was a catch in his throat — 'I cannot sing.'

I did not want to look at him. I did not want him sad. I was warm with the morning and something sweeter than his oils hovered over my face.

'*Lilyana.* Purple lilies of the riverbanks, with little flecks of white in their hearts, look,' he said. 'Newly opened but only for an hour.'

I did not know what 'hour' meant.

'Come, we must get to the rooms.'

Neither did I know what 'rooms' meant.

'There you can hide and rest,' he whispered, almost tender.

'Hide' I've always known. But not 'rest', never rest.

Eating and speaking are bound together. Eating unlocks the throat and the tongue.

'Seeds,' I murmured when he fed me a handful.

He clapped his brow, he clapped his hands. I thought he would not stop smiling. I thought I would not stop smiling. My first word: seeds. And in his language. So I could now understand and speak other tongues? I thought, it must be from going through the fire the second time.

'Seeds,' I said again.

'Yes, picked while you were asleep,' he explained. 'I'm so glad you can speak again —welcome to the Kingdom of Seeds, Amedea — Amedea, isn't it?'

'Yes, daughter of Abarama and Alkesta,' I whispered. So he had heard my name, perhaps when I spoke it as he rescued me from the fires, and now he remembered. He knew me, he knew me.

'These are the golden grains of *wirra,* meaning "from the sun".'

They were not the dry seeds from the rations. They were bigger and had moist centres. After a while, I had a sweetish paste in my mouth. 'Like eating and drinking at the same time,' I said.

'We'll be walking through fields of wirra. Eat as much as you want, Amedea.'

The grains were a precious comfort, but not as comforting as seeing him not sad. Not as precious as hearing him call me by my real name.

The fields of wirra were golden, as if the sun itself had come down to earth. I fed shamelessly, after my life of hunger. How could any place have too much food lying idle? I ripped the stalks and grains with my hands and teeth. Quickly I cleared a row of wirra, then another and another. There was no time for talk. All that the shocked Verompe heard was my endless ripping and chewing, not the whirring.

Verompe had to drag me away from the grains. For the first time I saw a trace of repulsion on his face, but it did not bother me. At least it was no longer inspired by my cursed mark. My brow was clean and I was happy enough, and he was showing me more flowers and explaining their colours, but the overeating had made me sick. I threw up on the red flowers then the blue ones, then the yellows and the purples. They became a blur as I fell on a heap of colours. Above me was also a blur as bright, hanging from the trees: more fruit, I was to understand. It was then when I heard laughter and the song I knew by heart, but only half of it. Someone was singing it over and over again, as if in search of the other half.

'The edge is a line, oh how lovely
It will stretch your eye —'

Quickly Verompe dragged me towards the thick grasses and clamped my mouth as I began to retch again. Just in time. The singer and her companion were about to walk towards the flowers where I had fallen.

'I love your voice, your mouth, but you shouldn't be singing unauthorised songs, not to my face — ah, girl, you have such pluck.'

'What's that smell? What happened to these flowers?'

I know this voice, but it can't be her! She has hair, short like a boy's but thick. I stared, I bit Verompe's hand. I wanted to call out to her who had risen from the grave.

Like me, Verompe could not believe what he saw. This can't be him! He can't be this grey and shrunken. Long ago he could lift and whirl him about in the air, so he used to believe he had reached the sky. He too wanted to call out to this man, but we should not be found out. He kept his hand clamped on my mouth.

'Wili, I want the purple this time — but what happened to these flowers? They smell wrong.'

I saw her cover her nose. Her hands were decked with tiny red flowers blooming from her wrist to her slim fingers, until they twined with her red nails.

'Yes, what strange and ugly smell, but don't worry, dear girl. Let's go where the flowers are thicker — '

'And where the fruits are sweeter,' she giggled, stooping down towards him. He was half her size. He nuzzled her breasts barely covered by a green dress with sparkly bits that trailed among the flowers. He was ancient but very strong. He lifted her, she laughed and threw her arms in the air. I saw her tiny feet sticking out of her dress. They were painted red which was also the colour of her lips. Redder than apple.

He whirled her about until they reached the thick flowers and trees where the fruits hung low and heavy. He picked a purple fruit, rolled it around his thumb and bit into it, then painted her lips purple. Then his open mouth came very close to hers, as though he would eat her — no he's singing, or was he? The song had no words. It was like the wind among the trees, the flowers, then it stopped as his mouth closed on hers for a long, long time. I wanted to see what Verompe thought of this, and if he heard the song at all, but I couldn't turn with his hand clamped tightly on my mouth. I could hear and feel his own breathing, which was quite strange, as if he were distressed.

When his mouth finally left hers, I saw that it was purple, seeking her shoulder. Was he going to eat it too? Then his hand crept inside her dress, and she giggled and sighed, and with each sigh the flowers around them grew bigger, brighter, multiplying into a whirl of colour, and I couldn't see them any more but I could hear ragged breathing then short gulps, as if they were dying. I wanted to scream but the hand on my mouth tightened even more, hurting me, and I could feel the pounding of his heart on my back and something else, something else, as the flowers trembled and I knew those two were dying and we couldn't do anything to help.

Verompe was trembling too, perhaps with the shock, I thought, and sweating hard against my back, which grew all wet, and it seemed his hand would never leave my mouth.

The edge is a line, oh how sharp

It will cut your feet

In my head, I heard the second half of the song that she had begun earlier, and I wanted to sing it to her, at least before she died, but it was impossible now. The flowers had buried Beenabe and the Minister of Mouths, and everything had grown very still in the Kingdom of Colours.

I was convinced that the dead could rise giggling from the grave. Before us they emerged from the flowers and unlocked themselves from each other's arms.

Her mouth wandered to his ear. 'Did it please you?'

'No, say it better, girl, say it like you mean it.'

'It pleased me,' and she giggled, stroking his cheeks as he gathered her waist. He barely reached it. Entwined, they looked like a strange tree.

'Here,' he said and laid a shiny drop of water on her palm. 'Wear it on my favourite spot — and here, your pass for the oils.' He gave her a red stone from his pocket. 'Pick up a new scent, something not too sweet.'

She smothered him with kisses, which he warded off reluctantly. 'I must rush to the Assembly.'

Her smile froze. 'Who is it this time?'

'Usual stray.'

'Was he caught?'

'*She* will be — it's a girl, a fascinating case. She sings and wears a mark, an insect of sorts.'

She went pale. 'Are you — are you sure?'

'Well, that's the rumour, but we're very keen to know her better. We've been monitoring her for some time. A locust on the brow? Yes, must be just a rumour, but one never knows — though I never thought she'd get here.'

Her knees gave way, but he caught her in time, laughing. 'Ah, I've pleased you too much, yes?'

'Are you sure — I mean, that she'll be caught?'

'Well, she's crossed the border, it seems — here, let me,' he said, pushing the sparkling drop of water between her breasts where it winked like a star.

We followed her to the Kingdom of Oils, as if we could follow the end of that conversation. The building glistened, proclaiming the richness that it held. It rose to an inverted V, which held up the sky or maybe pushed it further up. A tower, just as my father had promised, though he failed to say that it gave off every scent imaginable, some so strong, we could see it wafting out of the little windows. The sprawling grounds smelled as intensely with flowers much bigger and brighter than the ones we saw. Most bowed towards a pool that kept changing colours, sometimes blue, sometimes yellow and even red. On closer look we saw that the flowers were dripping thick liquid into this pool, and those that were too far away had a little catchment, which trickled the juices towards the pool. There were also animals that prowled around like furry blue balls on three legs, but gracefully and without disturbing the efficient arrangement around. At first I thought they were wearing yellow stones under their eyes, but I was wrong. These were vials catching the constantly dripping fluid. The animals were crying out their oils. And among all these were slender golden pipes sprouting from the earth like overgrown flowers or grasses. It was hard to tell how high they grew.

We saw Beenabe walk through this splendour and into the shining building. In her green dress and decked with flowers, she looked like the flower of flowers or the most unusual animal around. A glorious stray.

We waited for her to come out. We had not spoken since he released my mouth, which now felt bruised. My jaw ached. He avoided my eyes. He kept touching his throat, swallowing painfully. I wanted to ask him questions that I could not put together in my head. I wanted to wash again in the biggest water. My back felt sticky and I smelled strange. As he did. I imagined it was because of the flowers.

She had changed clothes, she had cleaned herself. She looked new as she walked out. Her steps were slow and heavy. She knelt before one of the furry balls. She stroked it, half crooning a complete song this time.

'Oh to find a gift — is it really one?
Oh to believe in the find —
Is it worth the belief?
Oh to hold worth in the hand!'

She sang it like a mourning song. Her voice was unsteady and could not quite rise to the high notes. She was in one of her damp moments. But unlike the blue animal now purring with pleasure, she had no little vial under her eyes.

They were silent and hidden. They were as green as the grass and they looked alike, those rows of little rooms. Late at night, Verompe sneaked me into one of them.

Earlier I kept asking him about Beenabe and her ancient companion, but Verompe only hugged his throat protectively. He walked several paces ahead of me. He brought me to a small pool where he demanded I wash. He waved me away when it was his turn. I heard him scrubbing furiously. He only spoke again after we arrived in the hidden rooms. 'For rest,' he whispered with immense relief, then he was gone.

It was too dark and I was too tired. Everything in the room felt soft and friendly, even the air. I closed my eyes for a long time.

So, a tree could grow even in a room. This was my first thought when I woke up. The tree was small, but it looked imposing in the middle of five bodies lying down. The three women and two men were censuring me with their eyes. Their paleness screamed against their long blue smocks that were just like mine. All had hands locked on their chests as if to protect them.

'I'm Amedea,' I said, then as an afterthought, 'I'm sorry.' I meant for crowding their small room. I wondered if they spoke my tongue.

They looked at me silently, my face, my hands, my feet, all parts of me that were not hidden by the blue smock. Then they closed their eyes again very slowly as if the act were a labour. Their brows knotted also as slowly.

'I'm sorry,' I said again, hiding my burns and wishing I could hide my face.

The room was lit by the tree's only fruit. Round and bright but not quite red. It helped me spot the tiny flowers almost hidden by the deep green leaves that looked like half-opened hands, which quivered slightly, making their own air. The more I looked up, the lighter I felt. I imagined I was in the open fields.

'If you look up, you'll feel better,' I told the others.

Beside me, a pale mouth twitched. It was raring to respond, but it seemed the act might sap the life out of it.

I felt something hit me on the cheek. Water? No, this was thick and dripping from the flowers above and it smelled familiar but not quite. This had no grit, it was all fragrance. Oil! It made the lying bodies move for once. Slowly, tiredly, they unlocked their hands from their chests. They released their hearts to catch each silent drop.

I could not bear the silence. Inside my skull it twitched, tuned into the rhythm of the dripping. Then I heard an old song, in perfect time with each drop of oil.

'So—soon— be—fore

The— si—lence— broke'

The silence broke further with the five hushing me and

dragging their bodies far from where I lay. Hands clutched at hearts again and eyes opened to censure me even more. 'I'm sorry, I won't hurt you,' I said, but all kept moving away from me and pushing against the wall, and I found myself slipping towards them. The room tilted with our weight and pushed the wall open into the next room where more bodies began pushing against the wall to get away from me and the song in my head. On we went, into room after opening room with its own dripping tree, with its bodies multiplying and slipping towards each other on the sickly fragrant floor.

Hands now covered faces, leaving only a little gap for the mouth to link with the next ear. The mouth to ear attitude stretched deep into the length of the room. All the rooms had become one long room where bodies were finally able to sit up and crouch against each other. It was like back in the ruins, only this place was solidly built and too well lit. It was overbright with leaves, flowers and fruit sprouting from the walls. The room buzzed with whispers in many tongues, but with only one rumour.

'Terror tired terror tired terror tired terror tired terror tired terror' made the growing walls tremble.

Why the tiredness? Why the terror? Is it *me*? I walked through the line of whisperers, apologising as I went. 'I'm sorry, I won't hurt you.' But their ears were only hearing the lone rumour, which after a while shifted.

'Border dream border dream border dream border dream border.'

My heart swelled. Did you dream it too? Did you walk

through it from a faraway place? Were you caught? Did you see the mothers' bloody hands?

I felt like I had come home. When I found the end of the line, I was ready to whisper my relief to the last ear, but the whirring in my head shut my mouth. Then the song —

'Sing how lovely, how deadly
Is your dream of the border'

'Lovely?' The whisperers rose as one. 'Lovely?' They were screaming now. Rage suddenly erased all tiredness and terror. Faces and hearts were bared, pushing me against the end wall.

'You think our terror is lovely?'

'You think our dreams are lovely?'

'You think our dead are lovely?'

'You think your song is lovely?'

The questions were chanted in time with fists pounding the air.

'No, I'm sorry, no, that's not what I mean — and it's *not* me, I didn't sing, please it's not me — '

'It's not me, it's not me,' they echoed bitterly. 'Children always say that.'

'I don't understand.'

'You do — you know how to play with our hearts. You know how to play with our dreams — '

'I don't — ' I began, but could not say more. I was blinded with sudden light and moving colours.

'Watch. First the fathers walked, then the mothers. Then they sent their children. The most painful betrayal.'

'A plague on our border!'

'A plague on our Kingdoms!'

Their voices rose with unbridled hate. Then suddenly, an explosion that shook the room. Lights, roaring lights! Lights, blinding lights! I couldn't see, I couldn't see. I thought I was back in the tent in our village, I was nine, I was burning.

'See? A child did that to us. How lovely.'

Of course, I did not see. I was on the other side. I did not see what they saw from where they stood — the moving pictures that played on the wall and my body, blinding me, afflicting my skin. Pictures of men and women walking to their border of trees. And then a child sneaking into the Kingdoms and among a crowd of tree worshippers. Just as they raise their arms, the child lights up, shatters. A great fire burns and burns.

'That's lovely?' the crowd spat out.

The fire played over me. I felt as if I was burning all over again.

'Lovely? Lovely? Lovely?' they kept chanting and moving towards me, hands outstretched, ready to tear me apart.

'We build fires to protect ourselves. We have done this since the beginning of time. Don't you forget that.'

'Father, do I ever forget anything you teach me?'

'But remember, there are good fires and bad fires.'

I wanted to tell about the fires that I had gone through to the two men conspiring before us. But hand clamped on my mouth, Verompe was as always strong and unbending. He had rescued me again, I don't know how. Maybe that final wall was pushed open with my fear. Maybe Verompe never left. Maybe he was among the chanting crowd.

'And there are good songs and bad songs.'

'I know father, I know.'

In the dark, the men's voices grew faint as they walked towards where I came from. To find me, Verompe explained as he eased his hold on me. 'Quxik and Xuqik. The son and the father. Quxik's my right-hand man at the rations, and he's a spy — as I found out — of his father Xuqik, the Minister of Arms. Ah, he'd wave those arms about and always have his way. But my father was not afraid of him, he sang and never let him win. That was a long time ago,' he sighed and grew silent.

I had a father too, a long time ago.

'You see, Amedea —' and he paused, unable to look at me — 'all sons have had illusions about their fathers.'

'Illusions?'

'Good dreams, very good dreams. Sometimes, only rumours. But we believe they're dreams, good ones, so we can sleep at night.'

I remembered my dream of eating pink prawns with Abarama. 'I thought — ' I needed him to hear me too, with all my dreams. 'I thought you were my father when you picked me up from the fires.'

Verompe sighed, hugging his throat again. He seemed to be hurting even more.

'Why do you keep saving me? Why the fires? Why Beenabe — and that old man? Why those rooms? Why their rage? Why the border? Why the desert and now these trees, flowers, fruit, oils and grains, so much of them? And none in the desert? Why you, why me? Why the children?'

'Why is terrifying.'

We had no answers, just some comfort in asking the same questions. I imagined he was also asking them in his head as we watched the stream of fires rising endlessly from distant towers. They looked like trees of light.

'Terribly beautiful in this Kingdom of Fires,' he breathed out. 'They're lit like that when everyone is safe in their rooms. Here the fear of fire is understandable, but no time to explain. We'll wait. Soon she'll take you to the safer rooms.'

She? But he refused to explain. We looked up for a long time. The fires did not hurt the moon or the stars. Most of them were hiding, because they could not outshine so much light.

I was handed over to my very first saviour. She wore a plain green dress and the winking star between her breasts. She was more beautiful without the other colours. I marvelled at her thick, black hair. I, of course, looked worse. I had gone through the fire the second time.

'They hurt you even more,' she sighed.

'I missed you, Beenabe, I missed you so much, as a breast would miss its heart.' It was all I could say.

She held out a hand then withdrew it. It was all she could do.

The rooms smelled of grass and trees, but none had trees standing inside. The 'green trees' were forever bathing, combing their hair (such beautiful hair!), rubbing their bodies with oils, or lying down with Kingdom builders who needed to rest. Here, whatever your colour was, it was called 'green', because you were fresh and supple. Whether you were a girl or a boy, your body was a pillow for dreaming away the cares of Kingdom building and all the labours that came with them. Only in these rooms could you dream with a colour different to your own. You could be joyful in impurity. It was allowed, but secretly and if it strictly preserved everyone's colour, which meant no children. Dream together then walk away alone.

Thus Beenabe explained her new home but without looking at me. 'Verompe brought me here, he brought many of us here. He picked me up in time, before I walked into the fire — when — when I saw my village burn.'

'But didn't that fire come from here?'

'What would you know — you don't live here,' she snapped at me. 'The bad strays brought the bad fires here long ago and burned trees and flowers and grains and the Kingdom builders, that's why they — we have to preserve *our* own fires. But these are good fires, our fires protect us.' There was pride in her voice. She was of the Kingdoms now. 'Here we live in natural beauty. We drink from the rivers, we eat from the fields, our colours are from the flowers and fruits, and also our oils. I can even sing now, but secretly, of course. My songs are not — the usual songs.'

I wanted to ask about the blue furry balls and why she looked so sad among them. And why *that* struggle with her ancient friend among the flowers. I wanted to ask about the star between her breasts.

She looked at me again. Her lips drooped a little. She asked me to turn around, examining my body. 'You can never be a green tree, but I can hide you. This is a secret place only for those who can be impure and yet remain pure, but what would you know? And why do you have to know? All that matters, Beena, is you're safe.'

'I know … I am not beautiful.'

She held out a hand, I believed to comfort me, then pulled it back, saying we should not be seen like this. I wanted to remind her that in the desert she held me close in her sleep, but she began to tell her story. She told me about the gifts of the

Kingdoms. She raved about the sweet oils on her scalp, ah how precious. They gave her hair, look! Her spirits lifted. She was almost affectionate. She asked me if her hair curled all right. She preened. I had no chance to tell my own story or to say I am not Beena. There was a knock on the door. A Kingdom builder needed to dream in her arms. She hid me in a box full of clothes that were as soft as her skin. I was to sleep there. I did to the loud dreaming of the man on her bed. In the morning, the dreamer rose and arrested me.

The room was almost bare and colourless, like water on its own. It had no doors or windows. The three ministers sat at a round table: Wilidimus, the Minister of Mouths; Xuqik, the Minister of Arms; and Ycasa, the Minister of Legs, a woman. A fourth chair was empty. I sat within a hole in the middle of the table. My chair went up and down and whirled, depending on how much the ministers wanted to see of me at any one time. Not that they had not seen me before or known of me. Minister Wilidimus had heard my songs years earlier. Minister Ycasa had known I was walking to the border. Minister Xuqik had arrested me after his night with Beenabe. He looked pleased with himself, rubbing his palms together in some secret delight. He had slept with his rival's favourite.

The ministers told me stories. All were hundreds of years old and proud of it. They were the oldest carers of the Kingdoms. They were the only ones who could manage peace and preservation, so they were bound to live forever. The Kingdoms could not allow them to die. Of course, there was so much to live for and to keep them alive forever.

'What with your secret visits to those rooms?' Minister Ycasa laughed and looked at the men with something between pity and affection.

Minister Wilidimus leant towards her, chuckling. 'Are you sure you've never walked to that part of the woods? Aren't you privy to all routes, even of dreams?'

But she only laughed some more, even as her cheeks grew red. 'I don't have to answer that,' she countered the accusation.

Minister Xuqik whirled his chair. Then they were all whirling their chairs as they thought long thoughts. They looked like ancient children. The weight of Kingdom building had shrunk them to my size and had whitened their hair. All wore it cropped short. Their shirts and trousers were colourless. They studied me with intense interest.

Minister Wilidimus had the keenest eyes and he smiled sometimes or maybe his mouth was itching to break into song. I recognised him. He was Beenabe's friend among the flowers. Did he know that I was also her friend and that I was arrested in her room? She was still sleeping when Minister Xuqik dragged me out. I could not wake her. His arms locked even my breath and he did this silently. Now he looked even grimmer beside Minister Ycasa who laughed all the time. She had the air of someone who wanted to play.

'What were you doing in those rooms?' she asked.

'I was sleeping.'

She laughed. 'You sleep too much. You slept a long time. Do you know for how long?'

She knows my story?

'Not history, Minister Ycasa, but the present.' The face of the Minister of Mouths lit up. 'Let's ask her to sing for us.'

'I don't sing, sir.'

'Oh you do, you do — I've heard you many times before and wondered — so give us a song, girl.'

They know my story.

'That's not why she's here, Minister Wilidimus, and you know that.' The Minister of Arms spoke slowly, making sure each word had equal weight, but the other man had no love for gravity.

'But my dear, doubting Xuqik, *the* singing is why we brought her here, or have you forgotten?' Wili retorted.

The Minister of Arms sat up. His hand had curled into a fist. 'Wilidimus, it was your boy who brought her here.'

'Uhmm ... I don't recall that at all, dear Minister.'

'Your bastard son brought you one of your pet singing projects.'

'Pet singing project? Aw, Xuqik, how dare you call it such? I am the Minister of Mouths, I know when a song is dangerous. Like the plague. Besides there are secrets in those songs only I can unlock.'

'Are they by any chance also the secrets of your favourite green tree, Minister Wilidimus — in your favourite room? And do you know where I arrested the plague?'

'Come now, dear, jealous Xuqik — '

'I am *not* your dear! And as you know, your *favourite* sings too — in secret.'

'It's not the singing but the walking that is the key concern, and that's my turf, gentlemen,' the Minister of Legs argued, all the while smiling indulgently at the men.

'I have collaborated with you, Minister Ycasa, and successfully.' The Minister of Arms smiled back at the woman beside him. 'You have designed the border and the routes for walking and running, and I make sure they are meticulously observed. I make sure those walkers do not plague us. You and

I know that the true plague is the fire that they carry in their bodies, and I make sure they never get anywhere near our border. But this man's chief of rations, this man's sprog had smuggled them through.'

'Oh, don't be peevish, Xuqik. Some strays are allowed in, the Kingdoms need them.'

'Use them, you mean. For guarding our trees? Minister Wilidimus, I have always opposed that stupid strategy of co-opting the enemy, of teaching them our caring values, of making them like us so we can feel safer. Rehabilitating them — is that how you call it? Hah! But of course you talked this policy into place and I have to deal with the consequences.' His fist was now pounding the air. 'You even talked the system into having strays keep your bed warm.'

'Only my bed?'

'And having them shoot vermin guris with arrows — to be kind to the earth, as you say — when we can wipe them out efficiently.'

'With the wicked little fires that you've concocted? Of course not, dear Xuqik. We do things naturally here, we live by the natural order. If you want to play with your fires, do it outside the border.'

'My fires protect the border!'

Minister Ycasa whirled her chair, laughing. 'I never get tired of your bickering, but we have to gather our natural bearings before *he* arrives.'

Her last words forced the men to give up their quarrel, though reluctantly. They whirled their chairs, they all looked up and quickly the ceiling opened as if their eyes had pushed it into the sky. The sun streamed into the room, striking colour everywhere. The ministers' clothes turned purple, their chairs grew leaves and branches and rose to the sky. They bore white fruit with a scent that was both gritty and aromatic. Ah, the oil of oils.

'Yes, let's restore the natural order, Ministers,' the woman laughed.

All sat high up on their own tree now, and began sprinkling it with a whitish powder that stirred an old memory. 'Blessed,' I heard in my head as the trees whirled and rose even higher into the sky. The powder was sprinkled beyond them and a field of wirra sprung from the floors and began ripening. My whole skull whirred, I felt the urge to feed, but my chair sprouted leaves and branches that bound me. I could not reach the closest grain. My mouth grew thick with saliva and something else that rose from my throat. I was retching even before I had fed. Then it broke out of my lips —

'A seed for a song, my dear
And oil to grease the throat'

I was singing? I was singing!

'What outrageous production is this — get down, all of you!'

The biggest head that I had ever seen emerged from the fields of grain. It looked up in dismay at his bickering ministers who whirled their trees about as if with some ill wind, then whirled them down, back to the level of the table. The leaves and branches drooped before the censure of the Honourable Head who sat on the remaining chair.

'You should be ashamed of yourselves.' The Head rested tiredly on his hands that seemed to be having a hard time holding himself up.

'Why? We're getting results. She sang and I think we're on to something,' the Minister of Mouths said, certainty in his voice. 'There are secrets in that song from the other side, secrets that need to be unlocked and monitored.'

'Why must we go through this circus? The plague was confirmed years ago. It didn't have to go through the border. Why was her route not blocked in the first place?' The Minister of Arms waved his fists about. The grains shivered.

'I have monitored all walkers, I have steered them away from here, I did my job!' The Minister of Legs thumped the table, sending leaves flying about. She was not laughing now. Had she not composed the Five Kingdoms' songs of transport and passage with precision?

'Ycasa, my dear, it's not you that's the problem.' The Minister of Arms glared at the Minister of Mouths who rubbed his throat before belting out the famous lines:

'No one should look

No one should walk beyond the horizon'

His song primed his speech. 'You see, I'm the one on your side, my dear woman. I have sung those lines with devotion, I've disseminated them to the world to assist your occupation, Minister — you have kept us all in our rightful place, with the aid of my songs, of course,' he said, smiling at the irate Ycasa. 'But I think our songs have been challenged — mocked and trampled upon at the other side, while *some people* simply looked on.'

'Some people?' The Minister of Arms was ready to hit the smug singer. 'I did my job, I dispatched the fires, you prick!'

'Watch your language, Minister,' the Honourable Head scolded.

'Yes, dispatched your fires to a village wedding? How heartless, dear Xuqik.'

'The signal was clear — they were walking to the border!'

'Shut up!' The Honourable Head finally silenced his ministers. The Honourable Zacarem was older than everyone and smaller, except for his head that thought for all the Kingdoms. It seemed to be aching with too many cares today. He buried it deeper in his hands. His next words were muffled by despair. 'What has become of you, of us?' But maybe I had misheard him, because my voice was finding its own words:

'If the feet itch for distance
Does the head know?'

'Do I know what — are you asking me, are you singing, girl?'

Everyone froze. I did not mean to interrupt him like that, but my throat had grown a will of its own. The Honourable Head was looking at me now, his tiredness quickly displaced by censure. No one had ever challenged him before. 'It is *she* who sings! Not that rumoured thing — not *that* mark. Where is it anyway? Where is your plague?' he asked.

The ministers argued in response, cutting the air with words that took me back to the desert. *Rumour. Plague. Border. Fire.* Stories jostled each other in my head. I saw my father walking under the stars. I saw the stars shot down, burning the earth to greater dryness. I heard rumours of water, of trees, of colours. I heard Inige's words. I echoed them. 'Rumour. The crime of hope.'

'What did you say?' one of the ministers asked the others.

'I didn't say anything,' the others chorused, then all turned to me. But I didn't say anything else again. I sang.

'Meet me over there
My left foot says to my right
Where there still lies
A wee quiver of life'

The Honourable Zacarem crawled onto the table to look me in the eye, or to find the missing mark perhaps. His censure shrivelled even the leaves and branches that bound me. He took my hand and we walked through the fields of wirra, leaving everyone behind as if they had never been there. The fields expanded with each of our steps. I fed as we walked and he watched.

'Have you fed on anything else?'

It was hard to answer between mouthfuls. 'Uhm ... sand ... locusts.'

'Tell me about the locusts.'

I felt the whirring inside my skull. 'Small and snug and hidden — but we still found them.'

'You remember that feeding?'

I nodded, not wanting to tell him that once I had forgotten everything.

Soon the fields of wirra became fields of trees heavy with fruit and pools of water reflecting all colours, and shy animals that hid behind the grasses. It suddenly hit me. So much abundance but hardly anyone to feast on it.

'Where is everyone?'

The Honourable Head smiled to himself. 'They're keeping the peace, they're preserving themselves at home. Thus preserving the earth.'

'But I don't see any homes.'

'They're hidden, they don't want to be disturbed after the festival. Yearly we pay homage to the trees then we rest. We let even the trees rest. We can't worry nature with all our to-ing and fro-ing. This is how to preserve it. We can't soil it every day with our want. We must return it to its purity, so we too are returned to ourselves.'

His purple clothes seemed to hang onto nothing. His body was barely there, except for his head. He was too shrunken, as if his flesh had crumpled into a slip of bones. But his words filled the fields, even the smallest leaf.

'There is a season for feasting.'

I knew it by his look. He was censuring me for feasting on the grains.

'But no season for wasting. Let me tell you about your ancestors long ago. They lived on season after season of feasting and fighting. They wasted the earth, each other and themselves, they were breeding beyond control.'

Aren't they your ancestors too? I wanted to ask, but instead found myself saying, 'I'm sorry, I didn't know — '

'Now you do. Their frenzy was beyond control. I had to think out a way to save this last green haven. I thought out the border between the wasters and the carers.'

'Who were they, may I know, please?'

'Isn't the answer obvious, girl?'

'But how do you tell between the carers and the wasters — how can you be sure?'

'I am *always* sure.' The emphatic way he spoke made the veins on his brow bulge and his cheeks tremble. Fire was in his eyes, then they grew dark.

His certainty filled me with terror.

'I'm always-always sure.'

I felt my cheeks burn then grow cold.

His hand swept through the landscape. There was pride in his voice. 'I re-thought this earth and found that it is good. First I stopped the wasteful fighting, I stopped the wars. I brought justice to all territories for the sake of peace. This quest was a difficult and bloody mission, but I succeeded. Then came purity. That was the best part. I purified the earth and our need for it. I controlled the seasons. Now there is a season for feasting, then for resting, and a season for just looking.' He ran his fingers through the length of a grass, a trunk, a leaf. He tried to reach out towards something moving behind the grass, an animal, he said, but it was too shy. I only saw a flash of black and brown.

'The gifts of the Kingdoms,' I murmured, remembering how Beenabe had told tales about them. I wondered if she knew where I was and if she cared.

'Precious gifts, yes. Look at how nature repeats itself in design. We can only repeat nature's law in the daily life of the Kingdoms. I thought this out, all of it. The buildings and roads of steel, all the unnatural trimmings had to give way to what's left of the water, the oils and the grains, the trees and the grass, and the very few animals that complete the gifts for everyone's eyes and stomachs. *For symmetry. For equality. For justice.* So the Kingdoms are more equal now. But equality is deserved only by those who are willing to care for these gifts. Gift giving is reciprocal.'

I was sure I had heard all those thoughts before, but I refused to hear the other memories that came with them. I desperately wanted to believe him, even if in my skull the whirring admonished my betrayal and forced me to ask, 'Tell me, please, why can't us strays be equal too — with you?' I choked on my last words, afraid he'd strike me for saying them.

The Head turned to me slowly, as if it bore the weight of all that anyone could possibly know. 'You are equal. Among yourselves on your side of the border — don't we give you rations equally? You are all equal only to what you have done to and for the natural world. Each is rewarded with what each one deserves. That's justice.'

'What do we deserve?'

The thin lips grew thinner as he smiled. 'Ah, you don't know the full story then.'

'What if we're hungry?'

He censured me again with those eyes. 'This is a season for only looking.'

'Why are the animals shy?'

His thin lips had almost disappeared, but he was not smiling. 'Shy? The animals are not shy but mortally afraid of our want — but what would you know?'

I know want, the desert knows.

'No animal is safe with the strays.' His lips curled in contempt.

I thought of the mothers feeding on the guris, I thought of hunger and I had so much to say but did not know where to begin and end.

'Let me show you something.' The Head tapped a tree trunk with his brow and suddenly it opened into a room of boxes of all shapes and sizes, walls of them. I stopped in my tracks. Not quite like the boxes from before. These were bigger, thicker. I waited for them to sing the Kingdoms' songs. I was sure these would have many voices with many highs and lows, what with their immense number.

The Head was studying me. 'Come in and tell me — what do you see?'

Closest to me were the thicker boxes with dark scratchings on the side. These were unlike the boxes that I knew. These smelled ancient and they were all colours. I wished Beenabe were around to tell me if the orange box that she'd lost looked like any of these. Maybe she could tell me what orange is.

'These tell all the stories about the wasters that made the animals shy, as you say.' He picked up one of the boxes, he waved it before me. It looked heavy with scratches even on its face. 'This is a book, these are walls of books, of stories and our commitment to them — ' and he echoed the Missions, while picking up one book after another. '*We will protect you* — the Book of Borders. *We will care for you* — the Book of Rations. *We will act for you* — the Book of Fires. *We will think for you* — the Book of Songs. They're all here, lest we forget them, especially the fires.'

Book? Box? Are the fires allowed to be told or sung? I stood there in awe, waiting to hear the stories. Now I'll know if I remembered right. Was it five hundred tents? Were they really blue? Did they burn for a long time, like the stars? But the boxes remained silent and he led me away from them towards even bigger boxes that I could see through. I stared at their insides. These I knew so well. Once I thought they were sticks and balls gaping silently at the desert sun. Now — they sing? Were they inside those other boxes all along? In the desert, in the ruins? I turned to him, overwhelmed by the shock of the possibility. 'Is it *them* that sing?'

'Of course,' he said, running his hand over a box that housed a skull and bones. 'In their silence, they sing. They remind us of history, they keep us vigilant.'

I faced a skull. I waited for it to sing, as I had I waited on the day I woke from my longest sleep. But from its gaping mouth, nothing. I turned to the Head, but he would have none of my confusion. He walked me through the long row of boxes and their silent skulls and bones. I waited and waited for the songs.

We stopped walking after the last box. He turned me around

to face where we had started. I heard more sadness than anger in his voice.

'All good Kingdom builders,' he said. 'All victims of the stray fires that had crossed our border — but never again, never again.'

'Do you know our stories? Do you wish to know them?'

The Honourable Zacarem did not give me a chance to answer. He was not even looking at me. He was pushing a wall of books, then he was pushing me down to my knees. I panicked. It had grown dark in the room, no, everything had turned black.

'You will not close your eyes, you will bear witness,' I heard him say.

How could I see? Around me, the walls had grown black. The black began to move. I thought I saw something emerge from the blackness. The black was breaking? Then the movement became an arm, a head, a torso. Then it hit me! A burnt body was rising from black fog and debris, then another, and another. Silently they began milling about, walking towards me. I opened my arms. 'Are you number 425? Or 500?' But they were just walking and never getting out of the blackness, never reaching me. How was I to know that they were the moving pictures of history?

I turned to Zacarem. 'Oh most Honourable Head, we were five hundred families, with blue numbers on us — to monitor our to-ing and fro-ing to the border— oh, yes, 1 to 500, sir — are they *them,* sir — please, was anyone saved like me?'

'Watch that blackness, girl. Your ancestors did that to one

of our biggest homes. The old and the infirm consumed in a second. Like kindling.'

I had never felt such dryness in my throat. When I found my voice again, the words were as dry. 'I didn't know, I'm sorry.'

'Yes … sorry … ' he whispered back.

Briefly we were bound in regret then his voice was restored to anger. 'We are the ones you love to hate, because we made it. We made good.'

'Blessed are they whose bones don't sleep
They are guarding the living'

Up and down the rows of boxes, my voice suddenly rose and fell like someone else's footsteps. I could not help singing. The urge came from my own skull: You bless all the dead, any dead, even if they're not your own.

The Honourable Zacarem seemed moved by my song. He kept muttering to himself, 'I thought so hard to fix the world … but maybe —' he looked away. 'Maybe I got it wrong.' Then he grew silent, his body easing, soaking up the song.

Did I hear him right?

The Honourable Head's eyes closed, lulled by my song. I sang to bless the dead, and the living breathed with the notes. This man of hundreds of years looked almost like a child now, in peaceful slumber. After a while, the corners of his lids grew moist. I reached out to wipe them, but then my song became a whirring and he quickly woke up from the lull. He looked around, uncertain, muttering to himself. 'But that sound — that's something else. *It* is something else.'

The whirring was unmistakable. He clapped his hands,

the place lit up. He grabbed me, examined my brow. 'What is singing?' The veins on his head bulged into a purplish map. 'Who is singing?'

The song rose with more vigour, but not from my mouth now. It repeated itself in between the whirring, then echoed further away in many voices. The Honourable Head dragged me around the room, he was shouting now. 'I should have believed the rumour — now girl, where is it, where are they?' His hands crushed my arms. 'It's out, they're out? Escaped to plague our Kingdoms — you're done with the fires, and now, locusts? My ministers will hang for this — they should have never let you in!'

'It's not me, it's not me,' I kept saying.

He clapped his hands again and the walls came alive, with moving pictures of the tired rooms, the terror room, the angry room, then the Kingdoms, as he chanted, 'Where are they?' He kept clapping and the pictures kept changing. He checked the sprawling fields of grain and trees, the flowers, the waters, the sky, then the border, which seemed curiously uninhabited. Where are its caretakers? I stared at this new picture. Outside the wall of trees, the fathers were drinking a woman's offered water. The mothers were laying pouches of grains and oil before another woman shimmering with lights, and a skull singing on her breast. It was *that* skull that we heard? The shimmering woman raised it. It kept singing in many voices, it finished the song:

'Blessed are they whose homes don't sleep

They are guarding the dead'

My friends had reached the border! I freed myself from my captor and leapt into their arms.

Where are Shining Lumi and Karitase, and the caretakers of the border? Where am I? I scurried around, searching for my friends. My head reeled with confusion. I was back in the rooms. I recognised the dripping tree and the tired men and women in their long blue smocks. Beside each of them was a pile of dry seeds like those from the rations. Many were eating, the others were rubbing their chests with oil. Their hands were gloved in amber fur. Those with eyes closed had lost the furrows on their brows. They looked rested and oblivious to my walking around. A few were still crouched in fear or raising their fists in anger but most had calmed down to the hand on heart gesture. Without the frenzy of bodies piling up from before, I noticed that they were huddled together according to the colour of their skin. No mixing.

Someone took my hand. Beenabe! She was also dressed in a blue smock. She put a finger to her lips and pulled me to a corner where three men were still linked in that fearful mouth to ear chain. I was forced to sit next to the last man and listen to the whispered, 'It's the fires, it's the fires.' Then she led me to other rooms where the fists did not have as much anger left in them. They were more playful, throwing the remaining seeds on the walls that were moving with pictures of strays walking to the border but never reaching it, because they had stumbled on fires that sprouted from the sand. At each explosion, a sigh of relief went around the room — those are *our* fires outside the border. Our fires protect the border. Then the familiar song of caution rose from the walls, but sang with no trace of warning now. It had become a lullaby:

'No one should look
No one should walk towards the horizon'

We had left the last room. We were crawling through the grass. Finally we could speak but only in whispers.

'You found me,' I said. I could not hide my elation. In my heart I knew she had searched for me. 'You did not give up on me, just like in the desert.'

This time she held my hand. We crouched together, taking in each other's face. It was like the first time she found me. I asked, 'What are they?'

'They're rooms for those who can't recover from the fires that crossed the border,' then on second thought, she added, 'No one ever does, really.'

I remembered how my village burned.

My friend echoed my memory. 'I never found our old hut. No trace.'

'I saw Zacarem's black wall, Beenabe, I saw all those burnt bodies — '

'Hah, the Honourable Head tells that well. That little orientation.'

'In those rooms, they look so tired.'

'With such terror and anger, how can they not be tired? But each year after the adoration of the trees, they rest. They're fed those forgetting seeds.'

'Like our rations in the desert?'

'No. Our rations are more potent, Beena. Strays are meant to forget their own stories from once upon a time, for good. So they won't attempt to walk to the border, oh it's hard to explain, but it's okay now, I'm okay now, see?' and she fluffed up her hair.

I wanted to argue that Cho-choli never forgot. But of course she never fed on rations because she never left her cave. And Daninen's and Espra's seeds were old and dry, potency gone, so they still remembered trees. Just as my father did, because our rations had stopped coming. But in Shining Lumi's tent, did everyone not remember? Did everyone not sing? Maybe we never forget after all. For how can we live now without before? How can we live before without after? But whose before and after can be told and sung? And who is allowed to sing — and when? Is there also a border for singing? The questions were whirring in my head, and only I can hear.

After a while, I asked about what confused me most. 'Why must our kind forget?'

'Safer for the Kingdoms.'

'But the old stories can't be forgotten. I saw walls of them, Beenabe. The Honourable Head showed me.'

Beenabe sighed. I sensed a battle inside her — between her wishes and loyalties, between her before and after. She could not meet my eyes as she explained.

'Those are *their* stories, *their* own devastation. All other stories and devastation must be forgotten, like they never happened. But not theirs, no, they never forget their own for good, even if they happened once upon a time. Here, they want only a momentary forgetting for rest. Because they're fearful that they'll forget and never remember, so they'll stop guarding the border, and they'll be unsafe again. It's mad. They have long memories here, Beena. Those fires crossed the border hundreds of years ago, but the ministers keep them burning in their hearts, so they're drying up, growing brittle with hate. They think the oils could help — or the new hearts.'

'New hearts?'

'From the other side, Beena.'

'What do you mean?'

'From the ration lines.'

We were quiet for a while. We remembered it well: the harvest of body parts under the blankets. The price paid by the strays.

'It's mad here, Beena, beautiful and mad, but I need my comfort, the Kingdoms' gifts, I deserve them,' she said, fondling her hair and the winking star between her breasts, then silence. When she spoke again, I heard the desperation for lightness. 'You won't believe this, I know now how *that* song ends. Remember the song at Daninen's and Espra's hut? I own it now.'

Our faces were so close. It was like sleeping together in the desert.

'Listen,' and she sang it to me. 'Remember it?'

I nodded, imagining the black, round animal spinning and spinning.

'I own the record now — and I understand. I understand now what it means to take love, Beena, and I understand how that song ends too —' and her face lit up as she completed it in a voice that spun joy in the air, joy that put an ache in my heart.

I listened long after her song had ended.

So is this what love means to you, Beenabe? The love taken is equal to the love made? But must love be reciprocal, for it to be love? You can't take it if you can't make it? Must love follow the law of the market? Like in the ration lines? Your last crockery for a fistful of seeds? Your heart for a jug of water? Your kidney for a vial of oil? But I kept quiet. I did not have the heart to puncture her joy.

'Ah, Beena, isn't the song so — so wondrous? It's like what

the Kingdoms say. *Justice.* You have to care to enjoy the gifts. And I do, I do all the time, in the rooms, oh how I love them all, I love even the strangers. They leave me with a gift of oil each time, they love me back, well, in their own way … so my hair grew. And I so love my hair,' she added, fondling again her most precious acquisition.

Such earnest declaration of love. Dear Beenabe, I loved you bald then, I love you with hair now, I love you even if you don't know my name.

'You'll hear all of it, the whole song, Beena, we'll play it when we get home — ' then she stopped, and finally sighed, 'No, you can't go home with me now.'

'Home,' I echoed.

The blacks of her eyes were so large.

'You *love* it here?' I asked.

'I need to survive, Beena, so I — we must hide you somewhere else, not in my room. You can't be seen there any more, I can't be seen with you, it's dangerous. I know it sounds — '

'I understand … I am not beautiful.' And I am not Beena, I wanted to add, but did this matter now?

Tentatively she touched my cheek. 'You do look better, though.'

Love is clumsy, because it has so many hands — I wanted to sing this to her, but it would not have mattered now.

She turned away. She had looked at my face enough, which mercifully no longer bore the cursed mark. Or maybe she was hiding her own face as she weighed *this* home in her heart. She fell silent again, then when she spoke, something else crept into her voice.

Ah, love. It has so many hands.

'But here, they blame — they blame everyone and everything outside the border. Their memories — they're like

— they're joyless.' She buried her face on the grass, as if she did not want me to hear, as if she was speaking to the ground. 'Their memories are joyless and unforgiving, Beena. They plague me, even — even when they're dreaming in my arms — when they love me for a night. Their cries of hate and terror mark my body, it's so confusing,' then she sat up, facing me, in earnest again. 'But of course they have to keep their memories awake to keep the border safe. To keep out the strays, except of course for a few like me — and as for the unwanted strays — oh, Beena, I can't let them do it to you, so we must hide you. Yes, that's what I mean, that's what I'm trying to say.'

'I don't understand.'

'No one does — look!'

From a distance, the towers spitting fire. The trees of light.

As the fires rose higher, the air grew a peculiar smell that made my stomach turn. I could not tell if I wanted to eat or retch.

'It's the worst time.' Beenabe had covered her nose and was urging me to follow her deeper into the thick grasses. 'I must hide you now.'

But where can you hide the likes of me?

Further away, the rows of rooms had suddenly lit up. The air smelled even more. We heard laughter. I looked at her, perplexed. What happened to the terror and anger? Are they better now?

Beenabe grew more agitated. 'After resting, they feast again. They'll have more than seeds now. They'll have meat, a rare treat, only once a year. That smell is from roasting animals — and — and people.'

'What?'

'They burn them there,' she whispered. 'The unwanted strays and even their own who can't abide by the seasons.'

I felt cold even while the towers heated the air.

'This smell, it's meat.' She nearly retched. 'Those fires cook the animals and burn the condemned bodies. At the same time. They can't be wasteful, especially with fire. An efficient arrangement, this dying and feeding.'

'But you don't feed on a grave.'

'I don't, it's them!'

We grew silent. Once I had fed among the skulls and bones and she hit me. 'You said you don't feed on a grave. You told me that in the desert.'

'I never did, I never did — and they're eating animals, not those bodies, I'm sure *not* those bodies!' The winking star rose and fell with her ragged breathing. 'It's the worst time, the worst time.'

What purity is there in time or in seasons, or in memory? This worst time evoked another and another. While sleeping together in the desert, my friend had mumbled in her sleep about another time when she had played truant, scavenging among burnt ruins. But her family forgave her. She always brought home condiments that made barley taste better. Once, the remains of a boy, though she never told them.

A grim time, but the mood was festive. The sky was like day with the fires from the towers and the lights from the rooms.

There is a season for settling scores. Quxik did not let us forget this. He knew the crackle of every leaf and every grass by heart.

He heard every whisper. He was thorough. He had followed us from the rooms. He eavesdropped on our distress. He was quick with his hands. I remembered the whisperers in the ruins as the bruise quickly spread on Beenabe's cheek. But he never touched me. I was his father's business. For my kind, there was another season for reckoning.

'Name the charges,' the Minister of Arms demanded.

The Minister of Mouths was more than willing. 'One, walking to the border. Two, singing. Three, feasting in the wrong season. Four, looking where she should not be looking. Five, disturbing the rooms. Six, spreading ill rumours. Seven, inspiring revolt among the border caretakers. Eight, sleeping in the impure rooms. Nine, bringing in the plague. Ten, contaminating the Kingdoms.'

The two ministers were not arguing now and the Minister of Legs was not laughing. The Honourable Head held himself proudly. They sat at the tallest table that I had ever seen, like a tower that rose almost as high as the ancient tree. Above them, the sky was an unstinting blue and the sun was warm.

The applause echoed again from the multitude that surrounded me. All were still dressed in their long blue smocks but none looked tired or fearful or angry now. Their faces were flushed as they chanted:

'What we work for is ours
What we care for is ours
What we protect is ours
Rejoice, rejoice!'

Here was joy claiming the sun, the sky, the trees, the waters, and even the ground where I stood. 'But we never took what's not ours,' I said.

'No one should look

No one should walk beyond the horizon'

The Honourable Head raised a hand to silence the crowd, then asked me, 'How does the Locust Girl plead?'

'I did not walk, I had no choice, I was taken to the border — '

'Border. Well then, let's talk about the border.' The Minister of Legs was in her elements. 'It is the protection line, the survival line. It preserves the last green haven on earth, because it keeps the wasters out. It controls the consumption of the last waters, the last trees, the last seeds, the last animals and the last oils for our survival. It is our last chance to preserve the human race from extinction. The border is our most precious invention.'

The following applause stirred the whirring in my head but only I could hear it. It could not compete with their rejoicing.

'Answer the question: How do you plead, girl?' the Honourable Head persisted.

'Hungry — I was hungry and — '

The crowd drowned my voice with their protests.

'Hunger. We can address hunger. I believe that subject is within my jurisdiction.' The Minister of Mouths pursed and stretched his lips several times before he sang —

'We are your keepers

We will protect you

We will care for you'

Then he made his point. 'The Kingdoms have taken care of hunger. We have managed ration lines for centuries. We have organised seasons for feasting. We have mechanisms for consumption and control. Hunger is a non-word now, except for those who wish to stir up resentment for their own vested interests — '

The Honourable Head raised his hand to arrest the minister's full flight into another song. Then impatiently, he asked again, 'Locust Girl, you know there's only one answer to the question — how do you plead?'

'I did not spread rumours, the fires are not rumours.' I thrust out my face to the crowd, I held out my hands, I exposed my feet. 'Look at me, I'm proof of the fires — twice I went through them.'

The crowd was silenced. The tiredness, fear and anger sneaked back into their faces. Quickly the Minister of Arms found his most soothing voice. 'Once upon a time, there were no fires and our forefathers were cold and vulnerable — then, in the darkness of one lonely night, the first spark was lit and our forefathers saw that it was good. Remember there are good fires and bad fires. So our forefathers gathered around the first spark and tended it until it grew into a fire that gave them warmth and safety to this day. Safety, protection, comfort. This is the good fire. This is what we build and keep in the Five Kingdoms to this day.'

The crowd shifted on their feet. Their hands crept to their breasts. *Fire* had been spoken. No story of comfort could erase the word from the air.

The Minister of Arms whispered something to the Minister of Legs who passed it on to the Honourable Head, who passed it on to the Minister of Mouths who shook his head in protest. The crowd grew more restless. The furtive exchange terrified them. They had never seen their protectors in this vulnerable mouth-to-ear gesture.

The Honourable Head cleared his throat. 'We need a witness to uphold due process of law.'

The ministers cleared their throats in assent, except for Wilidimus who was rubbing his in obvious discomfort.

From the trees further back, Quxik appeared. Behind him walked Beenabe now wearing the bright clothes of the mothers at the border. Arguments in different tongues erupted from the crowd. Is she another stray? No, she's one of the 'green trees.' Are you sure?

The ancient protectors of the Kingdoms raised their hands for silence and the Honourable Head said, 'We do what we must do for the right reasons: *Peace. Purity. Piety. Preservation.*' This calmed the crowd but only for a while.

Beenabe was made to stand beside me. I reached out to her, but she stepped back. She refused to look at me. Her clothes were in sad disarray, her precious hair unkempt. Like me, she had been locked in solitary confinement for three days before this trial.

The questions spilled in rapid succession. I could hardly follow who was asking them.

'What is your name?'

'Beenabe.'

'Where are you from?'

'The … room.'

'Louder.'

'The impure room.'

'Do you know the accused?'

Silence, then, 'Not really.'

'What does that mean?'

'I knew of her.'

'Of course — and when was this?'

'Once upon a time.'

'Where?'

Silence.

'Where, girl?'

'I don't remember.'

'Yes, you do. Where did you know the accused?'

'The desert.'

'Where are you from originally?'

Silence, then, 'The desert.'

'Why are you here?'

'For Kingdom building.'

'Louder — why are you here?'

'To help the kingdom builders dream.'

'What is the name of the accused?'

'I — I don't know.'

'You mean, you don't know her?'

'I knew … of her.'

'Did you know that she walked in the desert?'

'I don't remember.'

'Did she walk from the desert to the border?'

'I don't know.'

'Why did she walk to the border?'

'Because … I don't know.'

'Did you walk to the border?'

'No — I was taken to — '

'Did she walk to the border?'

'Maybe.'

'To hurt the Kingdoms?'

'No!'

'How do you know? Why do you know? Are you in this with her?'

'No, no!'

'Do the Kingdoms not take care of you? Do you care for the

border? Do you care for the Kingdoms' preservation? Are you not part of Kingdom building? Whose side are you in?'

'I am a Kingdom builder!'

Resentment rose from the crowd. No Kingdom builder is impure.

'Do you know the accused?'

'Yes.'

'Who is she?'

Silence, then softly, 'The Locust Girl.'

'The plague?'

Silence.

'From the evil fires across the border?'

Silence.

'Like you, of course — '

'No!'

Evil fires. The air crackled with it. The crowd's resentment deepened into something else that left me breathless. It moved towards us, towards her.

'You are from the side of the evil fires — '

'I'm not, I'm one of you — '

'You came to spy on us, and we clothed you, fed you, gave you refuge!'

'No, no! I'm on your side, I work for you!'

I tried to reach out, to put myself between her and the crowd, but they swept her away. Her cries kept ringing in the furthest corner of my skull.

I stared at her, at her brightness. But it was only much later that I understood *orange.* And the link between the word and the colour. The orange box that she had lost in my graveyard of bones. The orange clothes of the mothers at the border. Not as bright as red but it burned my eyes. Beenabe's dress was orange, now turning red and torn. When the crowd stepped back, all I recognised was her breast because of the winking star.

'Peel your eyes off me
I am not beautiful'

Who was singing? Was it the dead? Only I could hear it, though.

The men and women in blue stared at their hands in shock. They knew charred bodies but not blood. They were convinced they had never known blood in their hands. Further back, someone was pushing from the crowd. I heard a murmur, I saw a blue hem. I felt a hand on my shoulder. I looked up. His face was a blur. He picked up what he could of Beenabe. He walked towards the ancient tree. I followed the trail of red and orange on the grass. Then I heard him, the same voice that always cleared its throat before speaking but could not do so now.

'How do *we* plead?'

His query hung in the air.

'You are not in the position to ask that question.' The Honourable Head sounded shaky but set on restoring order.

'How do we all plead?'

'You're not to address me like that.'

'I am addressing my father.'

The Minister of Mouths cleared his throat repeatedly, as if whatever was lodged in there would not go away. 'Put that down, idiot! You've caused enough trouble.'

'All my life, I did everything you asked of me, even if you refused to see me again. I did everything that the Kingdoms asked of me, even if they refused to let me stay because I am not pure. I have crossed and re-crossed the border. My blood runs from both sides. I am contaminated. I fed the strays, I reined them in, I used and cheated them, I expelled and abused their children, as I had been expelled long ago. Father, I learned the trade from you: expel those who are unlike us, because they threaten our caring values, our way of life. Better still, exterminate them to preserve our peace. Does the other side have no right to their peace? No. Because their peace threatens our own and more legitimate peace?'

'Shut up!' the Minister of Mouths was choking with rage.

'I'm sorry. I should not be speaking in terms of *our* or *we* — I never belonged to you. You are born of these Kingdoms, you are pure, grand, heroic and sadly, mortally afraid. Your fear of the other side inspires your heroic acts — your ruthless songs, your terrifying fires.'

'Fire is not my department and you know that, you fool, you utter fool!' The Minister's rage was spilling into distress.

The son turned away and walked among the crowd, holding out Beenabe's body. Everyone shrank from it, hushed.

'I saw villages burn in my mother's desert, I knew strays who blew themselves up in my father's Kingdoms, I read all the books of devastation, I know the terror and tiredness in the hidden rooms, I saw fires that we planted sprout in the desert, I know the maimed bodies of children, the very few ones left, oh so well — oh how I used them so well. So who started the first fire? And whose is the devastation? Whose is the terror, whose is the hate? Does it matter now? A burning is a burning and a charred body has no face. And blood? Blood is red on both sides of the border. I am witness and victim and culprit, so I ask, how do we all plead?'

'I think we do not plead, Verompe. We offer, we love.'

I must have said that. Strange how we say things that we don't even understand at the time of uttering.

A trial must proceed. Prosecutors must return to their original villain. Finally the Minister of Mouths recovered his composure. 'Don't stall the proceedings, you idiot! I have gone through enough trouble to save you from yourself.'

The Minister of Arms chuckled. 'Too much trouble indeed. You have put duty on the line, Minister Wilidimus. You have known about your son smuggling strays through the border. You have compromised the safety of the Kingdoms.' He could not hide his satisfaction. Father and son had just owned up to corruption in public. 'How do you plead?'

'Don't muddy the waters, dear man. The Locust Girl is our case, or have you forgotten? We agreed to bring her in, to know why your little concoctions have lost their potency — why this girl remembers even the stories from once upon a time and why she sings those songs of revolt — why she survived the fires in the first place.'

'Listen, Ministers, there is a time for everything,' the Head pleaded.

'She can sing, she can remember,' the Minister of Mouths railed. 'She is proof that your forgetting seeds and your fires no longer work, Minister Xuqik. Your arms are useless! So how do you plead yourself? Who bungled his duty?'

'I said, there is another time for this,' the Head snapped at the men, but the Minister of Arms had already leapt onto the table and grabbed his rival's neck. 'You do not question my arms or my duty, loud mouth.'

'Fools, fools!' cried the Minister of Legs. The men were now locked in a full-blown fight. She could not prise them apart.

Verompe laid Beenabe at my feet. The crowd milled about, confused. Most were backing away from us, wanting to return to the comfort of the rooms. Some had collapsed on their knees from sheer exhaustion. All had hands on their hearts.

Suddenly a crackle, or was it a whisper? Did it start with the leaves, or was it only the grass? Whatever it was, it stopped the fight. It was ferried by a soft wind. Words, they were sang words.

'Please … fear … hand … '

For once, we were one in listening. The words were coming from the border. The Head and his ministers jumped to their feet. Xuqik had only one thought — the border caretakers! They were singing? His son was already rushing to find out.

'Seed … song … oil … '

Then more words in more voices singing together.

'Please have no fear and
Take this offered hand'

I recognised it — the song about Karitase and her jug of water! I felt for movement in my head. Nothing. Who is singing?

'A seed for a song, my dear
And oil to grease the throat'

The other song that exposed Shining Lumi's trade! Where's it coming from? All checked their neighbour's mouth, all were suspect. Meanwhile the two songs rose like an argument, each line parrying the other.

'Please have no fear and —
A seed for a song, my dear —
Take this offered hand —
And oil to grease the throat — '

The argument went on, echoed by the crowd also arguing now with each other, hurling accusations. You're singing! No, I'm not! You're from the other side! No, I'm with you! Hands clutched at hearts and throats, confirming innocence. All silent in here, they protested to themselves, even as the songs woke up a familiar cadence in their lungs.

I could not help it. I had to sing. I had to end all arguments.

The crowd turned to me, relieved. They had found their culprit. The unseen songs had found a body, a host.

I gathered all the unseen voices in my throat. It swelled with many more voices. Even my eyes, cheeks, chest, belly swelled, hosting voices from everywhere and everyone in all tongues. I sang a multitude.

'Please have no fear and
Take this offered hand
Your thirst, your thirst
Is my only affliction'

I was afflicted with song that would not stop.

'A seed for a song, my dear
And oil to grease the throat
Where I will find you safe
Breathing yet, breathing yet'

My body grew, pushed to accommodate all voices from all sides of the border, both desert and green haven, and I couldn't contain them. I couldn't bear the strain. I burst and caught fire.

I saw them watch my charred remains. I saw their horror, their fascination. They felt their bodies. Safe. They queried their neighbours. Safe. Then the trees. Safe. I saw their relief. The fire had claimed only *one* body. I saw them make their way back to their rooms, their rest and their dreams.

But how can I see when I am no more?

When all had left, the wind picked up and began lifting bits of my remains. It was then that I heard the faint whirring. Wind eddied around the site of the burning, as if to dig it up. It cooled me, and my back quivered. Fluttered. Then slowly it opened, spread itself, and suddenly I was airborne, risen from my charred flesh and bones.

Wings? I have wings!

So what am I now?

Who am I?

I began to answer, to assure myself, but all that spilled from my mouth was the whirring, then words, halting at first, then a song parrying the whirring and the wind, then rising above them in a melody never heard before.

'I am Amedea, daughter of Alkesta and Abarama
I am Beena, beloved of Beenabe
I am Locust Girl, kin to Cho-choli, Daninen, Espra
Fau-us, Gurimar, Hara-haran, Inige, Just-me-uhm
Karitase, Lumi, Martireses, Nartireses, Opi, Padumana
Quxik, Rirean, Silam, Trapsta, Unre, Verompe
Wilidimus, Xuqik, Ycasa, Zacarem'

Oh how sweet it is — how sweet to remember all who have touched us!

It was hard to leave. I went from one tree to another. I visited the fruit and the flowers and the biggest water. I hovered over the fields of grain, afraid to land. I memorised the colours, afraid I'd forget them.

Earlier, after my resurrection I basked in the sweetest song of my history even as apprehension then fear crept in. So what am I now? A locust with the heart and voice of a girl? Will I feast on these fields and raze them to the ground?

I flew into each Kingdom, each tower. I saw the glut of water, oils and grains. I saw the fires and what they did. I saw the remains of their own feast. How white those skulls and bones. How white the powder that poured into barrels marked 'blessed.'

When night fell, I visited them one last time in their rooms. They were turning in their dreams of a hand offering them a jug of water. How dry their throats, but the hand was afflicted with sores so they could not drink. They could remain dry like kindling and implode.

I flew over each one of them, lightly roosting on their rest, their dreams.

Suddenly a whirring began waking up in each of their brittle hearts and bones. It afflicted their eyes, their ears, their tongues, their noses, their skin. It fluttered into melody. It was no longer safe and snug and hidden.

'What greater plague is there
Than what we do to each other
What greater love is there
Than what we do for each other'

The melody was smooth, the texture of oil, but the words took longer to form. Soon the song spilled into their secret places, learning how to spread its wings. It wished to be known, and to know its sleeping host that did not know what it had hosted since the beginning of time. But knowing is slow, and it must grow in you.

'So, do you know now?'

Who is asking?

'And what is knowing but simply learning how to sing.'

Who is speaking?

Maybe it's the wind.

How they tossed and turned with this possibility of knowing, but only in their dreams — will they remember when they wake up? Who they are, what they are?

I visited the Kingdom of Oils one last time. Where I saw Beenabe crying and singing before she sheltered me in her room. I wanted to remember, to commit her song and tears to memory.

Tonight the Kingdom and its garden were lit by flowers of all colours. I saw again the blue furry creatures prowling on three legs and crying out their oils. All were lined up, a blue line trooping deeper into the garden and into what looked like its innermost chamber hidden by the tallest grasses and flowers heady with all fragrances. But one fragrance lorded over them. Aromatic grit so strong, it made me almost sick. As I flew in, I understood why.

In the middle of the chamber was the largest white bowl I'd ever seen, filled with oil to the brim that was encircled by a glistening blue. And afloat on it was Zacarem.

The Honourable Head sleeping in a bowl of oil.

I hovered, flying low.

The Head wore the saddest look.

Was he dreaming the saddest dream that no glut of oil could salve to rest?

Then I saw why the circle was a glistening blue. Seated on the rim around the bowl were the blue creatures quietly crying out their oils, filling it. My chest tightened, welled up, as I surveyed this saddest silence.

I came closer, very close to the rise and fall of Zacarem's chest. Exposed like the chest of the palest child. An open flower, with the ribs so defined underneath, like petals curved into himself.

I landed and began to cry, fluttering my wings, beating them against my body, against his body. Then something fluttered in response inside his chest. Like me, it whirred, no longer snug and hidden.

The Head shuddered, opened his eyes, and caught me in his hand.

In his terror-filled eyes, I saw what I had become. Tiny and winged with a locust mouth, but with the eyes of Amedea, of Abarama, of Alkesta, and the body of a girl crying on his chest, his hands, and into his eyes, as we stared at each other.

I cried into his dream.

Then just as suddenly as he opened his eyes, he closed them again and I flew out.

It was a good wind that night as I flew through the wall of trees. Just outside were the border caretakers who had left their posts. They looked peaceful. They were feasting on seeds and water, and rubbing each other with oils. Perhaps the seeds of forgetting were potent again, because the crowd was singing, they seemed happy. Perhaps with no memory of the fires from once upon a time. Such comfort in the loss of history. I felt both sorrow and relief. But my friends were not relieved of their tasks. Karitase was still offering her water. Shining Lumi was still showing off her skull. I hovered over their shadow and light hovering over what looked like bits of orange and red, with a winking star. Karitase was washing them with water, Lumi was salving them with oil. And the skull looked on, guarding the remains of my beloved Beenabe.

No one noticed me land on the winking star. Where her breast was, where her heart used to be. I sang to it her favourite song, but now our own.

Now the lovesong is sung, so the throat is as clear as the thought. But are you still listening, in your own chamber, your own ribcage, wherever you are?

Can you hear that little flutter?
It's an insect heart.
Too close for you?
Ah, in you.
Now you know what we've always shared.
No border can deny it.
It's small and snug, and not quite hidden.
Don't despair, it will settle. In you.
It will settle. Like the wind.
The wind is kind. It leads me home.

Look, a strange sprawl. No longer black and white as Beenabe spied when she looked beyond the horizon. The bones and skulls are gone. I feel the push and pull between finding and missing. It wrenches me apart. I remember the skull turned into white powder. I think of the barrels of whiteness that make trees grow.

Home, now a green stubble as far as the eyes can see.

Ah, dear Beenabe's barley seed three years ago. It's early days, but already I feel the urge to feed. I know our nature, I know our history. How we plague, how we love. How frail the heart, yet how enduring. I know because I landed on a winking star where her heart used to be, and it made me sing a new song.

I sing it to you now. Because it's such a long flight across the border.

'The love you take home
Is all my love, my dearest'